THAT BUZZARD FROM BRIMSTONE

THAT BUZZARD FROM BRIMSTONE

A WESTERN QUARTET

DAN CUSHMAN

FIVE STAR
A part of Gale, Cengage Learning

GALE
CENGAGE Learning™

Detroit • New York • San Francisco • New Haven, Conn • Waterville, Maine • London

GALE
CENGAGE Learning

Set in 11 pt. Plantin.

Printed on permanent paper.

LIBRARY OF CONGRESS CATALOGING-IN-PUBLICATION DATA

Cushman, Dan.
    That buzzard from Brimstone : a western quartet / by Dan Cushman. — 1st ed.
        p. cm.
        ISBN-13: 978-1-59414-690-9 (alk. paper)
        ISBN-10: 1-59414-690-X (alk. paper)
        I. Title.
    PS3553.U738T46 2008
    813'.54—dc22   2008027457

First Edition. First Printing: November 2008.

Published in 2008 in conjunction with Golden West Literary Agency.

Printed in the United States of America
1 2 3 4 5 6 7 12 11 10 09 08

TABLE OF CONTENTS

RECKONING AT ROBBER'S ROOST 7

THE GAMBLER'S CODE 61

THE CRAFT OF KA-YIP 141

THAT BUZZARD FROM BRIMSTONE 159

★ ★ ★ ★ ★

RECKONING AT ROBBER'S ROOST

★ ★ ★ ★ ★

I

The masked man had chosen his spot well. It was at the very bottom of Piegan Pass where the stage road dropped over a precipitous three-foot bank into the swirling waters of Elk Creek. Toward the pass this ford was concealed by a thick growth of fir trees, but in the other direction, toward Bonanza Bar, it ran straight as a rifle shot across a grassy clearing.

The masked man stood tall and straight. In spite of the blanket that concealed his body, there was something about his nervous, vibrant movements that marked him as young. His mask was a black handkerchief suspended from his hat, and through its slit eyeholes his eyes shone blue-gray and intelligent.

He listened. From above came the *clip-clop* of hoofs on rock, the grind of leather brake shoes. Minutes passed. The sounds would seem close, they would die out, and then emerge louder than ever. He crouched behind a boulder. With a sudden *clatter* the lead team swung in view around the fir trees. They hit the creek at a good clip, but almost halted as the coach lurched and groaned up the steep bank.

The masked man was on his feet, each hand holding a Navy six-gun.

"Reach for it!" his voice cracked out.

Both driver and guard were taken by surprise. And good reason—this was an incoming coach, a coach from the States, as Montana Territory still called her war-torn motherland. Road agents robbed outgoing coaches, the ones carrying gold.

9

"I have a friend up there in the rocks." The masked man gestured over his shoulder toward the twin muzzles of a sawed-off shotgun trained down from the projecting point of porphyry. A black hat and what seemed to be a portion of a man's cheek were also visible. "Don't make any moves he might misjudge. He's nervous on the trigger. You, inside!" He turned his attention to the craning passengers. "Don't show yourselves unless you want to be shot at."

"Is that so?" A girl's face spitefully appeared at the window. The eyes she fastened on him were dark, but filled with color, and fire. For a moment all the highwayman was conscious of were those eyes, but then he became aware of the beauty of her features, too. Her lips were parted a little, and her slim throat and shoulders were tense. "I'll look if I please," she went on, "and those two guns aren't going to stop me."

The masked man looked at her for a few seconds, then he gestured to the guard: "Toss down the strongbox."

The guard looked down on him for a moment and thoughtfully shot tobacco juice at the whiffletree. "She's a light one, lad."

"I'll take it." The box crashed to his feet. "Now get moving. And don't stop."

For emphasis, he fired one of his Navies in the air and the horses lunged forward. As the coach rolled past, he was conscious of the lovely face looking down on him from the window.

A second bullet from his Navy broke the lock on the strongbox. He seemed to know exactly what would be inside— two thick packs of Union greenbacks. The coach was now a hundred yards away, so he tossed off his blanket and mask, revealing a well-knit, angular body, and a young, rugged, and rather pleasing face.

He worked swiftly. First he concealed the greenbacks inside

his shirt. Then he retrieved the shotgun from behind the boulder up the hillside—there was no man there, of course, but the ancient hat hung over the abandoned bee's nest was a good enough counterfeit to fool anyone. The coach was just rolling from sight beyond the clearing when he led out his wiry little cayuse and put a foot in the stirrup.

"Young man, from some ways of lookin', that was a smooth job. But from others it was plumb awkward."

He spun around, hand streaking toward a Navy.

"I don't reckon I would."

He didn't draw, for there was something in the posture of the small, gray-whiskered man facing him that advised him not to.

"Thar, that's better. I wouldn't like you to commit suicide." The old one's gray-matted chin revolved thoughtfully around a chew of tobacco while his thumb remained as it had been—hooked in a belt loop just over the butt of a revolver. "Gettin' back to the original subject, you seem new at the business. What's your handle?"

The young man hesitated. He had almost blurted his real name—Tarrant Andress. Then he said: "Terry. Just Terry."

"Glad to know you. Forks gen'lly calls me Old Dad."

Terry had now recovered his composure. "So you think you could have done better?" He smiled.

"I didn't exactly say that. It was just that a few little points showed you up as a novice. F' instance, you shouldn't have tackled an incomin' coach. Why? The best you can get off them is greenbacks, and they're too easy to get caught with. Next, you didn't go over the passengers. Some of them pilgrims carry sizeable wallets. And last"—his eyelids drooped menacingly—"you're in my territory, and I don't like it."

Old Dad rubbed his gray stubble thoughtfully. "Still, I'm of a forgivin' nature and hate to see anny-mossity inside the p'fession. Besides, I've took sort of a likin' to you. I might even take you on as an apprentice if you hanker to learn from an authorized master."

"Maybe I would." Terry grinned.

Old Dad's shoulder moved just perceptibly, but, by some baffling legerdemain, a Navy had appeared in his hand. "Let's see them greenbacks."

Terry was desperate. It wasn't the money involved—it was that losing the greenbacks would spoil his carefully laid plans. However, if he could save a portion of them. . . . The desperation must have shown in his eyes, for Old Dad nodded.

"I won't take all of 'em. Fifty p'cent is my regular apprentice cut." He took one sheaf of the greenbacks. "Saddle blankets!" he growled. "They disgust me." But he looked satisfied when he pocketed them. "No hard feelin's?"

Terry breathed deeply. "None."

Old Dad then holstered his Navy and grinned. "Fine! Stick with Old Dad, and, barrin' accident, you may one day become one of the finest, most upstandin' hold-up men in the Nor'west."

He splashed across Elk Creek and appeared a moment later leading his horse. "It's a great life . . . no back-breakin' labor, no plowin', no seedin', no cultivatin' . . . just harvest time twelve moons out o' the year. True, the risk is extensible, but the reward is great. While they fit our failures with hemp cravats, our successes wear the finest silk. Terry, you'd be su'prised at our boys that have come up through the ranks to become wealthy and respected. Started out with nothin' but a Navy and a handkerchief, and retired as country gentlemen, even deacons and squires. We got 'em in gov'nor's chairs, and behind judge's benches, and we've sent 'em to the gleamin' halls o' Congress."

By unspoken agreement, they headed their ponies toward Bonanza Bar, and, while they rode, Old Dad lifted his voice in wavering song.

If Jay Cooke was only my maternal gran'paw

I'd have little Jenny Lind sing me to sleep,
I'd have San Francisco Nellie fry my flapjacks
And Gen'r'l Santa Anna herd my she-e-ep.

II

Bonanza Bar and its sister camp of Blackfoot were booming gold towns whose log shanties, tents, and dugouts sprawled along three or four miles of Missouri River terraces. No one could really tell where one camp started and the other left off, but there were two business sections, and, chiefly because it boasted the two-story stone building of the Hedges Enterprises, Bonanza's was considered the more metropolitan.

Terry unconsciously felt of an inside pocket when he saw that sign reading: *Hedges Enterprises—Lyon Hedges, prop.* Lyon Hedges! He was the great man of Bonanza Bar, and one of the great men of Montana Territory. He was also the nephew of Ramford Pierce, owner of the Rocky Mountain Stage Lines.

Terry had in his inside pocket a letter from Pierce addressed to Lyon Hedges, but he dared not deliver it—yet. It could wait. He had a more immediate goal, and he saw it now—a saloon emblazoned with a single word: *SHEP'S.*

"You goin' in Shep's saloon?" Old Dad asked with some surprise.

"Sure. He's a member of our profession, isn't he?"

"So I've heerd," Dad conceded, "but he ain't one I'm particularly proud of." Then in an alarmed tone: "You ain't one of that gang, are you?"

"No. I'm pretty much a lone wolf, just like you. But a fellow down Washoe way told me that Shep could get rid of watches and such truck that it might be unpleasant getting caught with. And these greenbacks. . . ."

"Say! If you can trade these shinplasters for good, gen-u-wine dust, take my roll, too."

Terry recognized Shep from a description the moment he stepped through the door—he was tall, stooped, long-haired, and picturesquely dirty. He looked Terry over without favor and made no immediate move to serve him; instead, he maintained an air of aloof arrogance as befitted one who claimed the eminent frontier station of saloon master.

Ten or fifteen seconds passed during which Shep chewed his tobacco on the right side, rolled it slowly to the left, and chewed it over there. Finally he spat on the floor and condescended to demand: "Yours?"

"Water."

The word seemed but faintly familiar. "You mean just plain chaser?"

"Water."

Shep overcame his original shock and glowered balefully. "Listen hyar, you! If you want to drink like a hoss, go down to the crick. . . ."

But he stopped and almost gulped his tobacco. He was looking down the potent end of Terry's right-hand Navy.

"I . . . said . . . water." There was a deadly emphasis on each word.

"Sure. Don't got cantankerous. Hyar, lemme polish up a glass. Now whar . . . Andy! Andy!" Andy was his assistant. "Whar's the glass? You cain't expect to water a gent'man out of a tin cup!"

After some scurrying around, the glass was found, polished, and filled with water. Terry slid back his Navy, at which Shep took a deep breath.

"I plumb mistook you for a pilgrim," he said apologetically, "and they ast for the durndest things."

The others in the room—three men who stood at the end of the bar—watched these proceedings with interest. Terry took time to look them over while he drank his water. He recognized

14

their type. They were what he pretended to be—they were of the wandering, lawless breed, the dregs of the West, men driven to each new frontier when the law arrived in the old, until here they were at the wildest and most lawless of all frontiers—the Northwest.

"Dakotah told me to come here," Terry said.

Shep started. Then a change came over him: his servility fell away and he became friendly. "Laws, why didn't you say so first off? Whar is ol' Dakotah?"

The last Terry had seen of "ol' Dakotah" he was suspended and swinging gently in the breeze that blew beneath one of Placerville's taller pines, so he was telling no lies when he answered: "Californy."

Shep nodded.

Terry finished his water. "I'd like to see you private."

"These boys is pure gold . . . a thousand fine."

"Private!"

"Sure. Come back to the little card room."

Shep's eyes became narrow when they fell on the greenbacks. "So it was you who tackled that coach. I just heerd she was robbed, and I didn't know as any of our boys was figgerin' on the job."

"Yes, it was me. I want to trade these greenbacks for gold."

"*Hmm.* I'd have to hunt up another party to see about that. Them saddle blankets is dangerous."

In five minutes Shep was back with a short, dapper man whose shrewd eyes seemed to have the faculty of seeing straight through a person.

"This is Cy Bender," Shep said.

"Just call me Terry."

Bender's thin lips twisted into a smile. "I hear you're the lad who kicked in that coach at the foot of Piegan."

"Right."

"And now you want to trade the greenbacks. Let's see them." He counted the money. "Twenty-five hundred. Not bad! I'll give you sixty ounces of dust for it."

"That's a pretty stiff discount. . . ."

"Take it or leave it."

"I'll take it."

Pleased with the deal he had just made, Bender broke down and became friendly. "I must compliment you, Terry, that was a good job. Lone hand. Maybe you could give our boys some lessons. You drifting on?"

"I might stay."

"Sure, why not? Maybe we can deal you in on some easy color."

Shep seconded the idea. "It's a cinch lay when you take cards in our spread, Terry. We'll give you protection, and. . . ."

"Shut up!"

Shep drew back before Bender's blazing wrath. "I only said. . . ."

"Shut up!" Bender thought for a while. "Well, now that Shep has mentioned it, we do have some connections that make our set-up better than most."

Terry smiled and patted the Navies at his hips. "Connections be damned, Bender . . . I make my own. But I'll stick around if there's real color in it."

Terry found Old Dad camped at the edge of the settlement. They divided the gold dust and prepared supper. When it came twilight, Old Dad declared his intention to "rest his wearies," but Terry had other business. He went back downtown and became a part of the throng that seethed, heavy-booted, bewhiskered, and profane, along Bonanza Bar's mile of saloons, gaming houses, and dance halls.

Here, under the lights of a thousand lamps, the raw, yellow

gold flowed across bars and green-cloth table tops; was lost, and won, and lost again; was spilled, tinkling, into pans of honest and dishonest scales; was cast to the winds, actually, so that industrious Chinese could be seen each morning waiting for the sweepings to gather the gold that had been dribbled the night before.

After an hour of wandering, Terry slipped up the side street beside the big, stone building that housed the Hedges Enterprises. He stalled in the shadows long enough to make sure that nobody was watching, then he entered the door. He asked for Lyon Hedges, and a clerk directed him to the second story.

The hall up there was dark, but a shaft of light came from one open doorway. He glanced in. It was an office divided into outer and inner rooms, and from the inner room came the sound of voices. A man was speaking—and then a woman.

The sound of her voice brought a sudden tenseness to his muscles. It was familiar. He had heard that voice just recently— but somehow he couldn't place it. He drew closer, but a board gave a loud *creak*.

Instantly the voice stopped. He quickly rapped, and in a second a massive, handsome man of thirty-five or so came from the inner room.

"Yes?"

"Mister Hedges?"

"My name is Hedges."

"Andress. Tarrant Andress, though I prefer to be known in Bonanza Bar as just plain Terry. I think this letter from your uncle will explain why."

Hedges opened the envelope and scanned the missive. "Well . . . so Uncle Ramford has taken a hand. So he's sent us a real lawman to stop these hold-ups." He chucked the letter in a desk drawer and turned the key on it. "I must confess I'm glad. Man . . . this road-agent situation is a blot on the name of the territory. A disgrace. You'll certainly get all the help you could expect from me . . . and more. Sit down, old man. We'll talk this over. Cigar? No?"

Hedges waited until Terry was seated, then he sat down himself and asked: "How do you plan to proceed?"

"To be exact, I have proceeded already."

Hedges's eyelids barely flickered. He leaned across to light his cigar by the heat that rose from the lamp chimney. His gaze didn't waver from Terry's face when he asked: "Just how have you proceeded?"

"I am the man who robbed the coach at the foot of Piegan this afternoon. On that coach was twenty-five hundred dollars in greenbacks. I traded them off for gold dust to Cy Bender at Shep's saloon."

"And what was your purpose in trading them . . . there?"

"To gain entrance into Bender's gang of road agents."

"Bender! Is he the one? You know, I've sometimes suspected him. A most undesirable character. But, man, if you know he's the leader of the gang, what are we waiting for?"

Terry frowned. "I haven't proof he's the leader. In fact, I'm convinced that he isn't. I think he's an underling. There's someone big connected with this . . . someone higher up. Bender would have no way of knowing when gold shipments are going out. Your uncle is certain that somebody has access to inside information."

Hedges looked at Terry through the rich smoke of his cigar. "Yes, Uncle is a smart one. But still, who could it be? All the gold shipments going out on the stage are handled through our office, and Charley Kibber is the only one with access to information. But, man, I'd stake my life on Kibber's honesty. Ten years a cashier with Overland, and two years with me, all without a blemish. Of course, there's young Tommy Romaine." Hedges cast his voice extremely low when he mentioned Tommy

Romaine. "But not him. Not Tommy. Why, he's George Romaine's stepson from Galena City. Those two, Tommy and Kibber, are the only possible ones . . . except me."

He thought this over for a moment. Then he laughed, and, as the thought seemed to gather humor, he laughed louder and louder. "Me! Ho-ho! Wouldn't Uncle pull down those spectacles of his and stare if you delivered me in irons? Wouldn't he? Oh-ho!"

Terry couldn't help warming to this robust, handsome man. He could see the reason for his popularity. Next territorial governor, it was said. . . .

Lyon Hedges drew an expensive silk handkerchief from his breast pocket to wipe away the tears of mirth from the corners of his eyes. "But back to earth. Those greenbacks . . . you said that was Uncle's idea. Now Uncle is a sly one, so I'd wager the greenbacks had some purpose beyond assuring your entrance into the gang."

"You're right. He thought it would be interesting to trace the bills."

"Oh-ho!"

"He thought the greenbacks might give away the gang's connections."

"They do have possibilities, don't they? But what are my duties?"

"You're to keep watch for any of them that come into the store. Jot down the serial number and who passes it."

"Is that all? Man, give me a real hand in this game. I might as well confess that I've always itched to be a detective."

"I think I'll take care of it quite well . . . alone."

"Alone. Man, I like you. 'Alone,' he said, just like that. Terry, you do things the way I like to see them done." He slapped his massive hand on his polished desk top. "You're my kind of a man. We could go places together, you and I. . . ."

III

Lyon Hedges's fine voice rang in Terry's ears long after he left the office. An unusual man—Hedges. A good man to have on your side. He had intended to go to Shep's saloon, but instead he found himself loitering around the side door to Hedges Enterprises. That girl's voice—it still troubled him. He kept trying to bring back the sound of it, and remember where it was he had heard it before. Then suddenly his inner ear heard that voice saying: *I'll look as I please, and those two guns aren't going to stop me.*

It was the girl of the stagecoach window. The recollection made him more curious than ever. He wondered who she was and what she was doing in Hedges's office. So he loitered in the shadow, puffed an unlighted cigarette, watched the side door. Soon he heard her light footstep on the stairs. She paused at the door until her eyes became accustomed to the night, then she moved away, her small boots *clicking* swiftly across the rocky ground.

Terry followed her. He did not skulk from shadow to shadow; instead, he tilted his hat to a careless angle, thrust his hands deep in the pockets of his homespuns, and hummed a little tune. She glanced around once, and that glance seemed to be completely reassuring. Even when he made the same turn along the main street, she did not seem to suspect anything.

She started to cross, but several long, jerk-line mule outfits blocked her passage. He drifted into a saloon and waited. The mule teams moved on, and she stepped lightly through the deep dust to the opposite sidewalk. She entered the office of the Big R Freight Line. He strolled from the saloon, crossed the street, roosted on a hitch rack, and smoked his way through a cigarette.

When she came out, he pretended to be interested in a noisy altercation between two muleskinners down the street, but he watched her from the corner of his eye, noting that her lips were set and that her brows were drawn in a troubled wrinkle across the bridge of her nose. He managed to mask his surprise when she walked up to him.

"Have you been hired to follow me?" she asked.

Terry smiled and doffed his broad California hat. He wasn't handsome, but his smile was a good one that had earned his escape from many difficulties in the past.

"No, ma'am," he answered cheerfully, "it was my own idea."

"It makes me nervous."

"I'm sorry."

"Especially nervous when the man following me happens to be a road agent."

Terry lifted his eyebrows. "What in the world can you mean?"

"I mean you should remove that hatband before you rob your next coach. Those silver ornaments are beautiful, but they are the sort of things a person remembers."

"*Hmm.*" Terry turned his broad hat around to examine the band from several angles. It was an excellent piece of Navajo craftsmanship and he hated to part with it. "You say this is beautiful . . . will you accept it with my best wishes?"

He only half expected her to take it, but she did, and with a pleased smile.

"How did you know I won't turn it over to Gus Stiver?" she asked.

"And who, pray, is Gus Stiver?"

"Our sheriff."

"I understand the sheriff here in Bonanza is none too effective."

"Perhaps you're right. The road agents certainly are getting bolder and bolder." She smiled a little, and there was a twinkle in her soft, colorful eyes when she glanced up at him. "They even pay visits to one of the territory's most prominent citizens. Only tonight one visited Mister Lyon Hedges."

"Then you knew I was there?"

"Yes. I recognized your voice from this afternoon. I was in the inside office."

"Did you hear our conversation?"

"I couldn't help it."

By common, unspoken consent they walked together along the plank and corduroy sidewalks that existed as evidence of Bonanza's civic enterprise. For the first time he noticed how small she was. Her head barely came to his shoulder, and the brim of her broad beaver hat kept brushing against his arm. He fell to guessing her age; she might have been anywhere from her late teens to twenty-three, or twenty-five. There was a certain poise about her, an assurance that proved her a full-blown woman. Her hair was dark and shone in the lamplight; it had been coiled beneath her hat, but some of it had escaped to fall in wavy masses across the collar of her little jacket. It seemed strange to be walking with a woman. There weren't many girls along the wild frontier—and few anywhere who could compare with this one.

"I'm Tarrant Andress," he said in belated introduction.

"Yes, I overheard that, too. As you see, I'm an unblushing eavesdropper. My name is Parcella Romaine, but my friends generally call me Pat."

Romaine! Lyon Hedges had mentioned a Tommy Romaine, stepson of George Romaine of Galena City. And, in mentioning the name, he had lowered his voice so she couldn't hear in the inside office.

"I've heard of the Romaines somewhere," he hinted.

"Perhaps in connection with the Big R Freight Line." She tilted her head and flashed a smile around the brim of her beaver hat. "You know . . . you followed me almost into the office."

"George Romaine, is he . . . ?"

"He's my father. He is . . . dead."

"I'm sorry. I hadn't heard."

Her voice suddenly became hard. "He was shot in the back two months ago. Since then, I've been general manager and agent, and I may end up by being chief muleskinner."

"But your brother. . . ."

"Hugh? He's away fighting in the Union Army."

"I thought there was a brother named Tommy."

"You've heard of him?" She smiled sadly. "I guess everybody hears about Tommy sooner or later. He's my half-brother. He . . . well, he liked to have a good time, so Father didn't get on very well with him. Tommy works for Mister Hedges."

The street wandered on, past stores and assay offices and saloons. Fiddles, concertinas, banjos, and an assortment of wind instruments blared from open doorways, mingling with the scrape of boots as miners danced with percentage girls at $1 a circle. Finally these places became fewer, and Terry grew conscious of the stillness that hung over the mountains. Although it was July, the air was sharp and cold, for, at Bonanza's altitude, warmth disappeared with the first shadows of evening.

Pat now told how her father, founder of the Big R, had chopped the first road over Piegan Pass and had sent over the first wagonload of provisions from Galena City. When more strikes were made, and its pay streams proved wide and rich, Bonanza became a mushroom metropolis, the great city of the territory. Wagons emblazoned with the Big R brand creaked day and night over the steep mountain trails. They hauled food and whiskey and mining equipment to Bonanza, and returned with high-grade gold in quartz for the stamp mills of California, and fabulous, peacock-hued chloride of silver ores that made the long trek to San Francisco by wagon, and thence by sailing vessel around the Horn to the smelters of Swansea in distant Wales. And then came the Circle S.

The Circle S freight line flooded the trail with huge new wagons. It cut rates and cut them again. Old customers of the Big R that could not be lured away discovered that their merchandise fell victim to Indian attacks with alarming frequency. But George Romaine had not been licked. Pat lifted her head proudly when she said that. He had sent his wagons over in great trains; he sought and won added financial support, and it looked for a time as though he might drive the hated Circle S from the trail. But George Romaine was dead . . . dead from a bullet in his back.

"And now you're running the Big R alone!" Terry made no attempt to conceal his admiration.

"I have friends," she answered.

"Like Lyon Hedges?"

She turned, surprised. "Why, yes. Mister Hedges has been very helpful. This evening he promised a contract to haul his freight."

"Who owns the Circle S?"

"A man named Dugan . . . Judge Dugan, they call him. But Father said Dugan was only a figurehead. You see, he wouldn't have the money to start a thing like the Circle S. He's just a drunken lawyer who came to the country with the Pike's Peakers."

Terry resolved to look up this Judge Dugan in the morning.

It was quite dark now that they were beyond the lights from the stores and dance halls. The road now wound between log cabins, pole and dirt-roofed dugouts, tents, covered wagons, then through an untouched clump of evergreens.

"What a dreary way to be walking with a road agent." He chuckled.

Only a hint of light penetrated the pine branches, so he sensed rather than saw her when she stopped and faced him. There was a rustle of the heavy silk she wore, and a stray beam of starlight shivered along gun metal. He hardly realized what had happened before the barrel of a double Derringer was being pressed beneath his heart.

"Just to prove to you that I need no protection . . . not even from road agents." Then she laughed, a low, rippling sound. "This is my traveling companion. I call her Annie. Perhaps there will come a time when I call on her for help."

The pressure vanished and he could hear her putting the gun back.

"However, the time is not yet, Mister Road Agent, and, anyway, we aren't so deep in the forest as you might suppose." He felt the warm pressure of her hand upon his arm. "Right there is the home of my friend, Maude Binkley. That's where I stay when I'm in Bonanza."

Maude Binkley's house was unusual in that it boasted a porch. Terry paused beneath its slant roof and said good night to Pat Romaine.

There was an extra spring in his step when he retraced his course along the street. He was strangely elated. He would help this girl. He would reveal this Circle S for what it was. He would help her lick them. Tomorrow morning he would drop around for a little, confidential talk with Judge Dugan. . . .

His mind filled with such thoughts, Terry was surprised how soon he was back to camp. Old Dad was propped against his bedroll, spelling out the words of a two-months-old San Francisco paper by the poor glow of the campfire.

"A paper!" exclaimed Terry. "Where'd you find it?"

"Over town."

"What does it say?"

"A pack o' things. The Union boys are raisin' tarnation down in the corn pone belt. Three Chinese was hatchet-hacked in a tong war . . . pesky critters, them Chinese. They'll be killin' some humans if this goes on. And, oh, yes . . . a promisin' young coach robber was found hangin' from a tree after he did some off-hand talkin' to an upper-level gal."

"Let's see that last item."

But Old Dad serenely folded the paper without seeming to hear. He yawned, stretched himself, and started pulling off his boots in an improvised jack formed by the crotch of a dead pine branch.

IV

Judge Dugan sat behind the battered, rough-board table that served as his desk in the office of the Circle S barns and looked Terry over without noticeable enthusiasm. Dugan was forty although long immersion in alcohol gave him the appearance of being considerably older. He was flabby with a lifeless flabbiness, his black serge suit was unpressed, his linen shirt unwashed, and his Windsor tie looked as if it had been slept in. A phlegmatic repose lay on his countenance, but his eyes were quick, small, and crafty.

"So you're a gunman?" Dugan spoke like the words made an unpleasant taste in his mouth. "What would the Circle S be wanting with a gunman? No, we have no need of your services, Mister . . . Mister . . . ?"

"Terry."

"What gave you the idea I'd want to hire a gunman?"

"Shep said something."

"Shep! He keeps his mouth going too much. A bothersome thing, a mouth. One finds how true that is when one practices at the bar. I'm a barrister, you know." Dugan threw back his shoulders with bedraggled dignity, an act that caused him to burp. "A Southern barrister, sir, disbarred by my contemptible colleagues because I espoused the cause of freedom. As a barrister I found that one should wag his tongue only when he is being paid for it." Dugan, warmed by his own eloquence, now became friendlier. "Truth is, Terry, we did hire some gun hands a while back, but things have been coasting along pretty well of late. But in case. . . . Anyhow, I'll keep you in mind."

A muleskinner kicked open the door and *clomped* in on dusty, horsehide boots. He was a powerful man, red-whiskered and heavy-jawed. He filled the office with the strong odor of horse sweat.

"How about my wages?" he demanded in a voice that matched his appearance.

"You should have been around yesterday, Hexum."

"I was, but you were too soaked to remember it." It wasn't the way an employee generally speaks to his boss, but Dugan didn't seem to notice. He thumbed through a notebook.

"Seventy-five dollars."

"Eighty-five," brayed Hexum.

"All right, then. Eighty-five. A man can make a mistake, can't he?"

Hexum grunted and splattered a large mouthful of tobacco juice across the unswept floor. Dugan rummaged through a tin cash box and came out with a sheaf of greenbacks that he started to count out.

"Not them!"

"Not these? Sir! These are banknotes backed by the might and wealth of the great government of the Union. . . ."

"I'll take dust. I worked until my voice cracked to earn that money, and I aim it should have some weight to it."

Dugan, grumbling, got out a small Chinese scale, suspended it on its silken cord, and weighed five ounces of dust.

"Hold on, thar," said Hexum. "That ain't Bonanza dust. That's Packer City dust, by the looks of it, and it ain't worth more'n fourteen dollars to the ounce. I want six ounces of that dust."

While Dugan and Hexum were arguing this point, Terry man-

27

aged to get a good look at the greenbacks. There was no doubt of it—they were the same ones he had traded to Cy Bender the day before. Not that it surprised him—he had suspected a tie-up like this. The Circle S and Cy Bender's road agents did business in much the same manner.

The muleskinner *clomped* away, and, after he was out of earshot, Dugan cursed him. The cursing stopped abruptly when Terry offered to buy a drink. At a nearby saloon he bought whiskies as fast as Dugan would drink them.

"Say, you're a good lad," Dugan wheezed after he had consumed the better part of a quart. He didn't notice that Terry still had his first drink in front of him. "Sir! I appreciate good company. A person like you, brilliant in conversation, versed in the arts." Terry was unaware that he had touched on the arts. "Ah, my young friend, be charitable with an attorney, disbarred by jealous colleagues. But what was it Shakespeare said? 'Judge not that ye be not judged. For the measure you mete, it shall be measured to you again.'" Dugan hiccupped and wiped a tear from the corner of his eye.

"Let's take a bottle and go where we can be alone."

"Indeed, yes! Let us take two bottles. These rowdy miners don't fit with my present mood."

Dugan led the way to his disheveled bedroom above the office in the Circle S barn. There Terry listened to long mouthfuls of Latin, to Shakespeare and Scripture quoted badly. Dugan also displayed a remarkable capacity for liquor. But, midway in the second bottle, Dugan reached his level and commenced to weep. Terry then knew his moment had arrived.

"Now this job we were talking about. . . ."

Dugan pulled himself together. "Indeed. A job?"

"You remember. You wanted a trustworthy man of culture to do some gunning for the Circle S."

"Indeed, so I did. Forgive me. Forgive a poor attorney who

has been crucified on the cross of social prejudice. I generally consult my largest shareholders ere employing men for confidential missions, but my judgment of human nature tells me you can be trusted."

"I'd be glad to wait while you asked Mister . . . Mister. . . ."

"Hedges."

Had the roof caved in, Terry would have been less surprised. Hedges! Why, certainly it was Hedges! He was a blind man—a bumbling blind man not to have seen it before.

Dugan went on, apparently not realizing the secret he had given away. "Indeed, my young companion . . . *nobis quoque peccatoribus famulis tuis parten.* I quote at random. Forgive me. . . . But don't you think we should have one more bottle . . . to seal a friendship so well begun. But stay! Here are a few drops still.. My friend, my dear young friend, forgive me if I weep. As it was said . . . 'Be not forgetful to entertain strangers, for thereby ye may entertain angels unawares.' "

"But about that job . . . ?"

"Ah, yes. The job. Extremely simple, sir. I doubt whether there will be anything in the wind for two or three days. But I don't soil my hands with trifles."

"However, I'd like to know. . . ."

"Peace! Peace!" Dugan hiccupped. "You merely dress like an Indian, whoop like an Indian, and burn a caravan of Big R wagons. Disgustingly simple, sir . . . and gratifyingly effective. But let us not speak of mundane things. Was it not Shakespeare who said . . . 'Lay not up for yourselves treasures upon earth, where moth and rust doth corrupt?' Let us speak of literature, sir."

"That was a good idea of Hedges to get rid of George Romaine."

"An unpleasant piece of business, sir, and one which I opposed. Stay within the letter of the law was my counsel. . . ."

Dugan paused to listen. Someone had entered the office down below. Heavy boots scuffed across the floor and paused. He cursed the interruption, then he got unsteadily to his feet, weaved through the door, and down the creaking stairway.

Terry could hear a mumble of voices. He walked to the head of the stairs to listen. Now and then a few words came up to him—"The Big R . . . Piegan Pass . . . about sundown." He tiptoed back to the room when Dugan's heavy step sounded on the stairs.

"There's business in your line, sir," Dugan said between gasps when he entered the room. He walked unsteadily over to the bed and sat down. "Big R caravan coming over the pass this evening. There'll be twenty of you on the job so there shouldn't be much trouble."

"Rob it and burn it, I suppose."

"Rob, sir? A plebian word. Let us not use it henceforth. We sally out, we attack the enemy, we destroy him, and we take what we have won upon the field. What else was chivalry but that?"

Terry smiled. "Chivalry had something to do with fair ladies."

"And here, too! If the knights of old rode to the enemy's castle and took the fair lady, our leader himself may do the same. As Cicero said . . . *et introibo ad altare* . . . or Moses . . . 'Give me that man who is not passion's slave and I will hear him in my heart's core.' " Overcome, Dugan arose and draped a heavy arm over Terry's shoulders. "As I do thee," he sniffled, "as I do thee. . . ."

Ten minutes later Dugan was sprawled snoring across his unmade bed, and Terry was thoughtfully leaving his office. His was a lone hand now. An hour before he had felt secure in the thought that Lyon Hedges, one of the territory's most influential citizens, was backing him up—and now, instead, this Lyon Hedges had proved to be the very man he was after.

Terry had to smile when he thought about his visit to Hedges the night before. *Wouldn't Uncle pull down those spectacles of his and stare if you delivered me in irons?*—and Hedges had laughed as though this was so far-fetched as to be utterly preposterous. Well, it didn't seem so preposterous now, even though Terry realized he was still a long way from winning. Thus far he had nothing except the word of a drunken lawyer.

Terry kept thinking about what Dugan had said about riding to the enemy's castle and taking the fair lady. The fair lady would be Pat Romaine. That was why Hedges was making a fine fellow of himself—giving the freight contract to her with one hand, and stealing back with the other. Then, when she went broke, it would seem that she owed him something. He suddenly hated Lyon Hedges. He hated him for the expansive hypocrite that he was; he hated him for his physical gifts, and for his education. And chiefly he hated him because of Pat Romaine. Then—as Terry was as ruthless in exploring his own motives as those of the men he hunted—a hard smile came to his lips. It was ridiculous, but Terry Andress was in love. Well, there were still plenty of chips to play—and his first play would be to prevent the attack that night at Piegan Pass.

Pat was not at the Big R office. He hurried to Maude Binkley's, but no one was there except the Chinese cook.

"I think Missy Pat she's go out with Lyon Hedges."

"When?"

"Mebbyso one hour. All same horse and carriage." The Chinese pointed in the general direction of Blackfoot.

Terry swore. It was two miles back to Old Dad's camp where his pony was picketed. He started off in that direction, but then he sighted a boy on a pinto pony and hailed him.

"Do you know Lyon Hedges?"

"Gee, everybody knows Mister Hedges."

Terry scribbled a note, gave the boy $1, and sent him off

with instructions to deliver it to the girl in Hedges's carriage. After watching the pony out of sight, he drifted back to the Big R barns from where he could see a considerable distance up and down Bonanza's main street.

He glanced at his watch. It was 2:00 p.m. Dugan had said the attack would be at sundown. Then there was still time.

He noticed three men ride casually from the rear of the Circle S barns across the way. Each was well armed, and each carried a bundle behind his saddle. He wondered about the bundles—oh, yes, these were supposed to be Indian attacks. No doubt the bundles contained the correct costumes. Two or three minutes later, a group of five came from behind Shep's saloon, riding in the same direction—and then two more.

Terry paced the sidewalk. Still no sign of Hedges or Pat. No sign of the boy on the pinto pony. Only the armed men, each with his bundle, heading in the general direction of Piegan Pass.

V

Pat Romaine had lain awake a long time the night before. It wasn't the bed—Maude Binkley had given her an excellent one, dry marsh grass stuffed into a canvas tick—but no matter how hard she concentrated on sleep, the more persistently did thoughts of Tarrant Andress fill her mind. She tried to think of the business that had brought her to Bonanza, of the crisis that faced the Big R Freight Lines, a crisis so serious that one more Blackfoot raid would spell complete disaster. She tried to think of the help Lyon Hedges was giving her, but the more she tried to think of these things, the more persistently did Terry Andress's reckless, smiling face return to haunt her.

In a way she was disappointed that he wasn't really a road agent. He would have been a perfect one—the kind of a person one dreams about but never meets in the flesh. But he wasn't a road agent—he was a detective, and detectives, in her dreams, were not reckless, smiling fellows like Terry Andress. That made it all mixed up, and somehow prevented her from sleeping. But finally she did sleep.

In the morning Lyon Hedges called. He talked for a few minutes and made an appointment to take her driving that afternoon. He excused himself and drove away after she told him about the Big R caravan that was due to make the trip over Piegan Pass that evening.

After Hedges was gone, Pat stayed near the front of the house, watching for Terry, but he did not show up. *He'll be around right after dinner,* she told herself, but he didn't come then, either.

At 1:30 p.m. Lyon Hedges's carriage rolled up. He handled his eager team of chestnuts with supreme mastery. He stepped down and bowed with expansive grace. This afternoon he was more carefully groomed than ever.

"How beautiful you are!" he exclaimed when Pat came from the door to meet him.

"Flatterer!"

"I'm perfectly serious. How could I be otherwise?"

"You haven't that reputation with women."

Hedges was perhaps pleased that he had such a reputation although he pretended to be a little hurt. He helped Pat to the carriage, followed her, popped his slim whip to send the chestnuts away at a brisk step. Then he said: "You wouldn't talk that way if you knew what a slave you have made of me."

His words surprised her—well, not the actual words so much, as the way he said them. There was positive seriousness in his tone. She looked at him with not unsympathetic eyes, then, without realizing what she was doing, she began comparing him with Terry. From every angle, Hedges had the better of it. He was more handsome; he had the grace of form and movement; everything he said, and his every act, marked him as a gentleman. But, still, it was Terry's face that she saw when she closed her eyes.

"You could make me very happy, Pat," he said.

"I don't understand . . . ," she faltered.

"You must know what I'm trying to say. I'm asking you to marry me."

Pat looked down and noticed how tightly her hands were clasped together. She didn't know what to answer. She didn't love Hedges—not the way a woman should love the man she married. But it had been difficult, fighting the battle of the freight lines by herself. This frontier country—it was brutal even for a man. How many times she wished she could just give up the fight, and marriage to Hedges would be such a simple way. He had plenty of money; he had the ability to extricate the Big R from its difficulties. If he had asked her yesterday, she might have answered, yes, but as it was, she thought of Terry Andress and hesitated.

"I worship you, Pat. I could make you very happy. We could go to New York on our honeymoon . . . to Europe. . . ."

It occurred to her that she was being ridiculous, thinking about Terry. After all, he had not even called that morning to see her. . . .

"Please say yes," he said, leaning close.

She was conscious of Hedges's manliness, of his strength as he bent over her waiting for her answer. It would have been easy to say yes.

The horses suddenly came to a sliding, pawing halt. Dust rolled over the dashboard of the carriage. The street ahead had been blocked by two wagons locked hub to hub. One of the drivers, a large, raw-boned man with curly black hair, was cursing loudly.

"Stop that!" commanded Hedges.

The curly man still cursed. Hedges listened for little more

than a second or two, then he wound the lines around the hand brake and stood. The curly man looked up and noticed Pat. He stopped cursing and fumbled to remove his hat.

But Hedges was now climbing down. He took a long stride. His fist swung in a half arc. It struck the curly man's jaw like a blow from a jackhammer, hurling him, limp and boneless, to the dust where he lay half under his wagon. A quick stream of blood dribbled from the corner of his mouth, forming a spreading, blackish spot in the white dust of the street.

Hedges calmly returned to the carriage. He unwound the lines, backed the team, and hunted out a passage between the freight wagons and the sidewalk.

"Now when we were interrupted. . . ." He smiled.

"Please!"

"Maybe you want some more time to think it over. That's all right. It was a little sudden, I suppose. I hadn't thought of that . . . you see, I've loved you for so long, have worshiped you for so long, that it seemed as though you must have known it. But I'll wait."

They left Blackfoot behind and were rolling at a quick pace along one of the low river terraces when a boy galloped his pinto pony beside them.

"Miss Romaine!"

Hedges stopped the carriage.

"Here's a note for you."

She unfolded the scrap of paper and read it. Hedges, showing no curiosity, gazed out across the broad Missouri. This boy wheeled his pony and headed back toward Blackfoot. She turned to call him, but he was beyond earshot.

"Can we go back now?" she asked.

"Certainly."

They rode for a half mile without saying anything. Several times she unfolded the note and read it. Finally she spoke.

"Lyon!"

"Yes?"

"Do you believe that a gang from here in Bonanza is attacking my wagons?"

"Nonsense! Who would do it? Who would want to . . . except the Circle S, and old Judge Dugan has neither the gumption nor the nerve. Believe me, your father was unfortunate in that he made enemies of the Blackfeet, and that's the one and only reason for those raids."

"This note . . . I shouldn't tell you, I suppose, but it's a warning that Circle S men are planning to attack the wagon train I have coming over the pass this evening."

"Nonsense! Utter nonsense. Who would write you a thing as that?"

"Your own detective."

"Andress? Do you know Andress?"

"I met him last night after leaving your office."

"He's a fool."

"No," she answered with strong conviction, "he isn't."

"Surely you don't believe him."

"I'm not sure . . . but I'd like to talk with him, anyway. He says here that he'll be waiting in front of the Big R barns."

Hedges had little to say during their return, but he recovered his usual hail-fellow front by the time he pulled the team to a stop at the sidewalk where Terry was waiting.

"Good afternoon, Terry," he boomed jovially. "What's this I hear about you sending letters to my fiancée?"

Fiancée! The word struck like a club between his eyes. Terry shot a quick glance at Pat hoping for a denial. She flushed and bit her lip. To Terry, her perturbation was a sign of assent. He quickly recovered himself. "You're a lucky man, Mister Hedges."

"I agree."

Pat didn't know what to say. Hedges's unexpected assertion

had momentarily robbed her of speech, and now Terry's nonchalance piqued her. She wanted to deny being his fiancée, but the opportunity didn't seem to come.

Hedges was speaking: "Andress, I understand you have been worried about the safety of a wagon train that Miss Romaine is sending across the pass this evening."

"That's true."

"Where did you get the notion that white men were dressing up as Indians and doing that sort of thing?"

"From one who wanted me to take part in tonight's raid."

"Nonsense! Utter nonsense!"

Terry spoke softly, and with a smile, but there was pointed significance in his words: "You officially subscribe to the Blackfoot theory, Mister Hedges?"

"Theory! Theory, man? They have been seen, I tell you! The survivors all recognized them as Blackfeet."

Pat placed a restraining hand on Hedges's arm. "Lyon . . . it was I who put that idea in Terry's head. Perhaps I was wrong, but I never thought those men were really Indians. And Father always maintained they were white men employed by the Circle S."

"That idea is most certainly wrong."

"I'm a trifle surprised that you feel so strongly on the point." Terry smiled.

Hedges stopped. Red anger flamed over his face, and his big fists knotted until the knuckles showed white. But he controlled himself, and even managed to produce a tight-lipped little smile. "Feel strongly? It's just that I don't like to hear those murderous Blackfeet hair-grabbers defended. I say the quicker we stop dealing with them, and trying to make treaties with them, the better. This country will never be safe for civilized people until they are wiped out. They're a scheming, no-good lot, all of them. They hated Miss Romaine's father because of some injury they believed he'd done them, and consequently each Big R wagon was marked for destruction from that moment on."

Terry addressed himself to the girl: "Believe me! No matter what Mister Hedges says, your train is in danger of attack by a group of twenty white men dressed as Indians."

"And I say it is not!" Hedges's voice cracked with the sharpness of a bullwhip. He stood, and for a second it seemed that he would lose control of himself. "Understand me, Andress, I say it is not! And I'm willing to let tonight's happenings prove that I'm right."

"You mean we should get a posse together and ride out there to see for ourselves who's making the attack?"

"I do not! Such a trip would be a waste of time, for there will be no attack."

Terry was surprised. Why had Hedges stated it in such a way? But perhaps he didn't know that the Circle S gun crew had already left for the pass.

Hedges went on: "If the attack takes place"—he emphasized the *if* and laughed to indicate how ridiculous such an idea was— "if it does, I'm willing to admit that I'm wrong and you're right."

"But Miss Romaine's wagon train?"

"I will pay all damages out of my own pocket."

With this announcement still ringing in the air, Hedges flirted his whip and sent his fine chestnut team prancing down the street. He turned the corner by his large, stone building.

Terry was suspicious. He climbed to the left of the Big R barn and watched from the bay door. He was there no longer than a half minute when a man rode away from the rear of the Hedges Enterprises. He rode nonchalantly, keeping his horse at an easy canter, casually swinging his quirt. But when he reached a fringe of trees along the hill trail, he spurred away at a rattling gallop in the direction of Piegan Pass.

"Mister Hedges, you are right," Terry muttered to himself. "There will be no attack on the Big R train tonight."

As he turned from the hay door, the *crack* of a pistol made him pause and listen. Not that gunfire was much cause for surprise in Bonanza—it was the direction of the report that made him wonder. It seemed to come from the Circle S barn. He waited, but there was no excitement over there, no sign of life. He dismissed the incident from his mind.

When he climbed down the ladder and approached the barn door, he saw Cy Bender stroll from the Circle S office. Bender paused to light a cigar and look nonchalantly up and down the street. Then he walked casually, almost too casually, in the direction of Shep's saloon.

Terry waited until Bender was out of sight, then he found a place at the counter of a little grease-smoked restaurant where he feasted on buffalo tongue and—oh, rare delicacy!—a genuine baked potato. He was topping this off with a dish of stewed dried peaches when Cy Bender came in.

"Terry, old boy! I've been expecting you all day. Why haven't you dropped in at Shep's? Or aren't you interested in that easy color we were talking about yesterday?"

"What's in the wind?"

Bender glanced around, and then spoke in close confidence. "As you may know, the express line has been taking gold to Salt Lake City by way of Piegan Pass. But that route has become warm of late, so now they're trying a new wrinkle . . . it's going to Fort Benton by way of Last Chance. From Benton it goes on to the States by steamboat." He paused for effect and leaned closer. "Terry, there's a shipment going out tonight."

"Fine. How many ways do we cut?"

"Five."

"I'd like a chunk of that. Where do we do the job, anyway?"

"At Three Finger Rocks, east end of Mule Shoe Cañon. The

coach is due to pass there just about sunup. We'll start from Shep's at midnight."

Terry watched Cy Bender walk away with his precise, quick stride. He could see the pattern now. He was to be involved in a hold-up, captured, and legally hanged. Thus, should Ramford Pierce investigate the fate of his detective, Lyon Hedges could explain it as merely a piece of bungling on the part of the unfortunate detective himself.

Terry hunted out the sheriff's office. Gus Stiver, Bonanza's elected officer of the law, sat with dusty boots hoisted to the edge of a table, picking his teeth with a pine splinter. He was a short man, thick-shouldered, ignorant but cocksure. He listened suspiciously while Terry introduced himself and explained his mission.

"So, you're a detective!" Stiver snorted.

"Here are some papers that should prove it."

Stiver looked over the papers at the distance he would have given the black plague. "Reckon they look all right," he admitted.

Terry kept trying to explain, but at the end of fifteen minutes Stiver was as suspicious as ever. So Terry left. He stepped into a saloon to watch. It was only a couple of minutes until Stiver hurried past, bound for Hedges Enterprises.

There was still one man who could help him—Commissioner Jonas. Terry knew nothing about him except that the camp had elected him judge—in this instance, a glorified justice of the peace. But Jones was not around.

Something tells me this town is going to grow slightly warm, Terry said to himself as he picked an out-of-the-way route toward camp where he hoped Old Dad would be waiting. *Just slightly warm!*

VI

Old Dad was nowhere in sight. The ashes of the campfire were white and cold. To kill time he stirred up a batch of biscuits. He stood up, listening. Two pistol shots, one close on the other, had split the evening air. Several minutes dragged by. Unexpectedly Old Dad sauntered in by a side trail.

"Hear the shooting?" Terry asked.

"I should have heard it," Old Dad answered significantly.

"What do you mean?"

"I mean that I just disposed of an enemy I was heretofore plumb unaware of. Stranger. He upped from behind a tailings dump and let fly at me. Bang, just like that. He missed."

"But you didn't miss."

"Missin' ain't a habit of mine, son."

Terry was thoughtful as he watched Old Dad go about the business of reloading the empty chamber in his Navy. Finally Terry remarked in an offhand tone: "I guess it's only fair to tell you . . . that fellow probably mistook you for a detective."

"Me?" Old Dad's amazement was such that his jaw relaxed, and for a while he forgot to chew. " 'Scuse me, lad. My hearin' ain't what it used to be. Wax in the ears, I guess." He chuckled. "For a second I thought you said I was mistook for a detective."

"That's what I did say."

"Oh, fiddle-dee-dee! How could I be mistook for a detective?"

"Because you're teamed up with me."

Dad's eyelids dropped a bit, but aside from that he seemed to digest the significance of these words quite calmly. "Proceed."

"I," said Terry, "am a detective."

"Then why ain't you arrested me?"

"I said detective, not sheriff. I was hired to come here and break up a certain ring of road agents. It just happens that you're not one of that ring."

Old Dad had finished his reloading. He inserted a cap, gave the magazine a roll, cocked the hammer, and then calmly drew a bead on Terry's forehead. But a moment later he released the hammer and tossed the Navy to earth with a gesture of disgust.

"Guess I'm gettin' plumb missionary," he grumbled.

Terry spoke on as though nothing had happened. "I'm going to need your help."

"Now hold on, young man," Old Dad warned. "They's an end to all things."

"I want your help and I'm going to get it."

Old Dad spread his hands and addressed the surrounding jack pines: "Waal, glory be, I really think he believes it."

Terry thereupon gave a full account of things at Bonanza Bar. He was sketchy concerning lots of it, dwelling mostly on the fight that Pat Romaine was waging against the Circle S. He kept an eye on Old Dad, noticing that the longer he talked, the faster and more vindictive became Old Dad's tobacco chewing. Finally the old man could contain himself no longer. He retrieved his gun and railed out with a blast of righteous expletive.

"The dirty thieves! Imagine 'em treatin' a pore young gal like that. I'm favored toward wipin' 'em out, plumb tee-total." He stamped around impatiently. "Waal, what are we waitin' for? I'm a man of rapid and dee-structive action once I get my mind set. Look to yore primin'! Whar's that Texas Derringer o' mine? Yipes . . . hunt yore holes, you ring-tailed civet cats, hyar I come, ridin' on the side o' the law!"

"Not so fast. We want to be sure and clean out the whole gang."

Old Dad was doubtful. " 'Course, there's only the two of us. . . ."

"That's why we need a plan. You see, once Hedges finds out

42

that Dugan tipped me off this. . . ."

"Who?"

"Judge Dugan. A drunken. . . ."

"Waal now, I don't reckon this Dugan critter will do much talkin' any more. Dugan is dead."

Terry recalled the shot he had heard from the direction of the Circle S barn, and the appearance of Cy Bender soon after. It was all plain now. Hedges had guessed it was Dugan who blabbed. Well, it didn't change the picture much.

"Dad, here's what I want you to do. It's a four-hour ride, more or less, across the range to Last Chance. There's a fellow there named Thaddeus Flynn. . . ."

"*Hmm,*" Old Dad pondered. The name Thaddeus Flynn seemed to be familiar to him—unpleasantly familiar.

"Ramford Pierce assured me I could count on Flynn if things got to running too rough . . . which they have. I want you to carry a message to him. The boys in Last Chance have been taking plenty of punishment from this gang of Hedges's, and Flynn and his vigilance committee will gladly accept an invitation to draw up a chair and take a hand."

"And you figger . . . ?"

"On having a little surprise ready for Cy Bender and his boys when we stop that coach in Mule Shoe Cañon tomorrow morning. Now, there's no time to lose. If you get to Last Chance by midnight, Flynn can have his committee together and be on hand at Mule Shoe in plenty of time. But an hour might make lots of difference."

Old Dad chewed it over. He started to say something, then he thought better of it. Instead, he asked: "What if my pony busts a leg? What if somethin' goes wrong? Do you have an idea what Hedges has cooked up for you?"

"Certainly. I'll be captured red-handed in the act of highway robbery. I'll be brought to Bonanza and tried before Commissioner Jonas so everything will be legal, and then I'll be hanged."

"Unless somethin' unforeseen should sway this lad Jonas in the meantime."

"What do you have in mind?"

"Nothing. Not a thing."

Old Dad caught his pony, saddled, hung a sawed-off shotgun to its horn, and thrust a Jaeger rifle in a scabbard under the animal's belly. In addition he carried a Navy at each hip, and in his belt was a Texas Derringer and a Hudson's knife. Thus well armed, he took Terry's note, waved farewell, and cantered from sight.

If Jay Cooke was only my maternal gran'paw,

he sang as he disappeared among the trees

I'd have little Jenny Lind sing me to sleep. . . .

Terry sat on a windfall, rolling and smoking brown-paper cigarettes, waiting for night. This gave him time to do a little thinking. His situation, while admittedly tight, still had some advantages. For instance—time was against Hedges. Every minute that Terry lived was an added menace to him. That meant Hedges had to act quickly. In view of that, he was surprised that Hedges had decided to let him live even until the following morning. He wondered about Pat. Hedges would probably get her out of town so she couldn't interfere with the hanging. This thought made him stir himself—he hurried to Maude Binkley's. She told him that Pat had left half an hour before.

"With Hedges?" he asked.

"No . . . it was with some stranger and I didn't get a good look at him."

"Will she be back?"

Maude wiped her dough-sticky hands on her apron and shook her head. "Laws! I don't know. She just ups and goes without tellin' a body nothin'."

Terry looked for Pat at the Big R barn. No one there had seen her. He stalled around, watching Hedges's office. No activity. He turned up the street.

Bonanza Bar was busy as always. Every honky-tonk teemed with heavy-booted men outnumbering by five to one the short-skirted percentage girls. Men stood in close, interested clusters around faro and roulette games at the Gold Road, the Eldorado, Katie's, and scores of lesser establishments. Terry looked with mild interest in the doors as he passed. He seemed casual in bearing, his step unhurried, but beneath this easy exterior his senses were rather fine. And he had gone only fifty or sixty paces when he sensed that someone was following him.

His pace remained the same. He scratched a little place behind his left ear; he whistled a fragment of a tune. He pretended to be interested in a saloon, but his eyes looked back. He saw the man then—one of the road agents who had been standing in Shep's saloon the day before.

He took the lay of the land. At his right were buildings in a solid row. At his left the hitch racks and the teeming street. He walked on, thirty paces, forty paces. Up ahead was a path that struck off between two buildings. That would be a good place to give this fellow the slip.

Up ahead a man who had been lounging against a hitch rack roused himself and took one step toward the middle of the walk. It was Cy Bender.

Terry moved to the outside of the walk. Someone started toward him from the opposite side of the street, paused at the rear of a freight wagon, waited.

For that second Terry felt like an animal standing on the trigger of a trap. Bender was going into a half crouch. The man behind him had stopped. The one in the street was waiting. For the space of a second, only Terry was moving—only Terry and the pedestrians who jostled one another along the crude pole sidewalk.

Two drunken miners came arm in arm. They sang "Sweet Betsy from Pike". They avoided Bender, and then lurched in front of him. Terry leaped for an open door. Gun flame lashed at him from the man at his rear. The bullet *thudded* close. Halfway through the door, Terry's own gun smashed an answer. But he had no time to ascertain the effects of his marksmanship.

He was inside a building. It was a barbershop. A half-lathered customer sat up, and the barber stared, brush in hand. Three strides carried Terry beyond a curtained archway to the barber's bedroom, and a moment later he was outside.

It was much darker here, in the rubbish-filled alley, than on the street. He paused for a while until he could see where he was going. Men were running through the barbershop. Terry dropped behind an old barrel just as two men came from the rear door. A few seconds and three others followed.

Bender's voice: "Hold on a second. He's here some place."

Terry didn't risk looking, but the voice sounded right at his elbow.

"What's that over there?" Bender had spotted someone moving beyond the alley near a clutter of cabins. They moved away, but Bender's voice could still be heard: "Wing him if you have to, but don't kill him. The boss wants to keep him alive . . . for an hour or two."

The scrape of their boots died away. Terry slipped through a saloon, and on the sidewalk out front he came face to face with Sheriff Gus Stiver. Stiver wheezed in a manner that indicated he had run a long way. He stopped, retreated a step, and something flashed in his hand. Terry didn't realize what Stiver

46

was about until the gun was covering him.

"You're under arrest," wheezed Stiver.

"Under arrest! What for?"

"For murdering Judge Dugan."

"You're making a fool of yourself, Stiver. . . ."

Stiver laughed, a raucous, confident laugh. "I reckon I ain't! I ain't so slow, Mister Gunman. You was the one what tried to make a fool of me, but it didn't work. All that hogwash about you bein' a detective hired by Ramford Pierce, or Jeff Davis, or somebody! Well, it didn't fool me for a second. I went right straight to Lyon Hedges and asked for myself. He pretty quick told me what you was . . . a road agent and a gunman. Well, you'll get what's comin' to you in our court, I reckon, and that mighty sudden . . . just as soon as we get Commissioner Jonas to hear your case."

Terry could see the pattern now. Hedges had decided against saddling him with the robbery—the murder of Judge Dugan would serve his purpose just as well. He had no doubt there would be enough evidence cooked up to convict him.

"The jail's right yonder and the first corner to your left," Stiver said, prodding him with the muzzle of his pistol. "And you better walk peaceful, because it wouldn't hurt my conscience to set this cannon off."

The jail was a tiny, single-room building made of massive logs. It had only one window, unbarred, but so tiny a child could not have wriggled through. The door was made of plank in two layers, and it was so heavy that Stiver had a hard time pulling it open with his free hand.

"Here's your office, Mister Detective," he said smugly.

Terry felt around in the dark until he found a place to sit—it was a bunk covered with dusty hay. There he pondered his predicament.

It looked bad. Not that he hadn't been in tight places

before—he'd been in plenty of them, but always before he'd had some card up his sleeve. Not this time. Old Dad was at that moment riding to Last Chance. Pat Romaine had probably been lured out of town.

He rolled a cigarette, but, having no way to light it, he had to be content with puffing the cold tobacco. Stiver had gone over toward Main Street and it seemed quiet for a while. Soon the medley sounds of Bonanza's night began emerging.

Farther away he could hear the *squeak* of fiddles, *twang* of banjos, and a woman's voice raised in music-hall chant. The song went on for many verses, then male voices chorused approval. Forlorn, like the cry of a prairie wolf, a clarinet wailed. Then a new sound—distant, fragmentary. It brought Terry to his feet with nerves tense. He listened. It came closer.

If Jay Cooke was only my maternal gran'paw. . . .

Old Dad! Terry wanted to shout his elation. But then a sudden fear clutched his throat. Why hadn't Old Dad gone to Last Chance? Had he reconsidered and decided he'd be a fool to help a detective? The song became closer, then it faded away and was lost in the night.

In a few minutes Stiver returned, a lantern swinging from one hand. He lifted it and peeped through the window to make sure Terry was still there.

"Did you get your orders from Hedges yet?" Terry asked.

Stiver sat on a packing case near the door. Half a minute went by before he answered.

"I don't take orders from Hedges nor nobody."

Terry laughed.

"Waal, I don't! And neither does Commissioner Jonas. We run our offices without fear, favor, nor prejudice. I'll guarantee you this . . . as soon as we locate Jonas, you'll get a fair, square trial, and after it's over you'll be given the benefit of a strong rope and a good drop."

A foot *cracked* a twig off in the darkness. Terry sat up, listening. He wondered if Stiver had heard it. But perhaps it was nothing. Stiver went on.

"Yep, it'll be a fair, square trial. . . ."

"You can't hold a trial without a prisoner!" It was Old Dad. Terry leaped to the window in time to see him approach, the light from the lantern glimmering along the gun-metal surface of his Navy.

"What the devil . . . ?" Stiver came to his feet, reached toward his gun, reconsidered, and stretched his arms high over his head.

"Open the door, lawman," commanded Old Dad. "This here's a hair-trigger and delay aggervates me plumb nervous."

Stiver leaped to do as instructed. He made three or four jabs with the key and nervously turned the lock. The door *creaked* open. Terry was there waiting to get outside. He lifted the sheriff's gun and stuck it in his belt.

"All right, Sheriff," Old Dad commanded, "git inside thar, pewter badge and all." He locked the door and threw the key far off into the darkness. He then apologized to Terry as they walked away: "I didn't reckon it would be healthy for me to take that trip to Last Chance. Night air has always been hard on my lungs. You see, Terry lad, I happen to be personally and unpleasantly acquainted with a couple or five of that Last Chance vigilance committee. I'm sort of afraid they might want to present me with a cravat . . . one of them adjustable kind which is guaranteed to last a lifetime. Howsomever, the way things played out, I reckon it's just as well for your health that I remained here. Do you forgive me?"

"You bet I do," Terry answered fervently. "But I'll wager you had some plan of your own up your sleeve."

"Now you mention it, I reckon I did. Fact is, I learned of

your incarceration by the merest accident . . . the accident be-ing that the sheriff yonder was all over town braggin' at the top of his lungs. You see, I stayed around to have a chat with that gal . . . Pat Romaine. She's a go-fetcher, ain't she? You bet she is! Why, I wouldn't be surprised if she gave both of us a lesson in detectin' before the night was out."

"Where is she now?"

"Either seein' Commissioner Jonas, or puttin' the thumb-screws to that worthless half-brother o' her'n. You know . . . Tommy Romaine who is in so thick with Hedges. Seems she's suspected him for some time."

Old Dad had an extra pony. They mounted and started along the alley. After they had gone forty or fifty yards, Stiver began beating his fists on the plank door and shouting for help. In answer, Old Dad aimed a warning shot through the window. The shouting ceased as suddenly as it had begun. Old Dad yawned.

Terry was impatient. "Let's get over there."

"Over where?"

"To Tommy Romaine's."

"No need. Miss Pat promised to meet us behind the Big R barn. I wouldn't be surprised if she was thar already."

But Pat was not at the barn. They waited. At last, even Old Dad became impatient.

"Son, I reckon we'd better find that gal. You ride out to Tommy Romaine's cabin, and I'll sort of keep watch here and over at Hedges's place. You can't never tell what that varmint might do."

Tommy Romaine's cabin was located at the end of a winding trail down by the river. A light shone behind the curtained window, but there was no answer to Terry's knock.

He opened the door. The room seemed to be empty, although someone must have been there only a few minutes before, because the odor of cigar smoke still hung in the air. A double Derringer lay on the table. It was Pat's. He strode over and picked it up. Then his eyes fell on the body of a thin, young man who was sprawled on the floor beyond.

He was sure this was Tommy Romaine. There was something reminiscent of Pat in his features, although his were weak while Pat's were strong. He bent over, listening for a heartbeat. There was none.

Terry stood, his eyes once more falling on Pat's Derringer. He was relieved to discover that the gun had not been discharged. But the fact frightened him, too. If Pat hadn't killed her half-brother, then somebody else had been there to do it.

Looking around more carefully now, he saw a cigar lying on the floor. It reminded him of the cigars Hedges smoked. He took the candle outside. The dust by the door held the fresh imprint of narrow carriage tracks—and the pointed prints of a woman's boots.

The carriage had turned near the cabin, it had followed the trail to a side street, it turned toward Blackfoot, then turned again, and this time headed back toward the big, stone building of the Hedges Enterprises.

VII

An hour earlier, Pat had said good bye to Old Dad, and had started out in search of Commissioner Jonas. She chanced to find him at a grocery store. Jonas was a tall, shrewd man— shrewd enough, perhaps, to have already guessed some of the facts about Lyon Hedges, the road agents, and the Circle S. He listened to Pat's story, and, when she was through, he nodded grimly.

"If the things are as you say, Miss Romaine, I'll do all I can to give those road agents something to think about. You go ahead and pump your half-brother, then look me up and tell me what you've found out."

So she hurried along the crooked trail to Tommy's cabin. There was a light, so she knew he was home. She rapped.

"Who's there?" It was Tommy's high-pitched voice.

"It is I, your sister."

"Oh, Pat! Come in." He opened the door and tried to act pleased at seeing her. He was a thin young man, colorless, shifty-eyed.

"I didn't come here to lecture you."

"Sure. I know. You're not that kind."

"I came here to find out what you know about Lyon Hedges."

He winced as if she had quirted him across the face. "Why, Mister Hedges is just my boss. I'm . . . well . . . I'm just a clerk in his store. You know as much about him as I do."

"He owns the Circle S. You were aware of that."

"I . . . well, I couldn't see it would do any good to tell. Honest, Sis, I would have told you if I'd dared, but he knows enough about me to put a rope around my neck."

"Tell me what else you know."

"I don't know anything else. On my honor! I knew he had some money invested in the Circle S, but I just happened. . . ." He stared with the color draining from his face while Pat calmly drew her double Derringer. "W-what are you going to do?"

"Tommy, my father died because of the Circle S. I believe that. And now he's trying to murder somebody else. Legally murder him." Her voice was suppressed, but it had a quality that seemed to vibrate in the small room. "He's trying to murder the . . . the man I love."

"Sis?"

"And you'll tell me what you know, or I'll. . . ."

"No! Don't shoot! I couldn't back out once I was in with him. I didn't know Dad was going to be killed until it was all over. Then I had to pretend it was all right with me, or I'd have got the same thing. But the Circle S isn't all Hedges is mixed up in. He's been sending gold out on stages for Cy Bender and his gang to rob. But he double-crossed Bender, too. He'd never send all the gold. He kept some out. He has it stored in the strongbox at the Enterprises building. Thousands of ounces. I've seen it there, in two leather satchels. Then this detective came . . . this Tarrant Andress. He got Judge Dugan drunk and found out everything. So Hedges sent Cy Bender to kill Dugan, and tonight they got the idea of saddling Andress with the crime."

Although Pat was hearing what she already believed, she could not restrain an exclamation of amazement. She let the gun fall to the table.

"I'm sorry, Sis. I really didn't know what was going on until it was too late." He covered his face with his hands. "Oh, but I've made a mess of things. I'm just no good. . . ."

The door that had been an inch or two ajar now swung slowly open. It made no sound and neither Pat nor Tommy noticed it until the candle flame fluttered in the draft. Pat uttered a startled cry when she turned and saw Lyon Hedges standing there.

He was frigidly polite. He smiled, bowed, and tossed away his expensive cigar. "I believe I was the subject of a discussion," he said in words like chipped granite.

Tommy faced around, his limbs atremble. He tried to speak, but only a wheezing rattle came from his vocal chords. What color he had drained from his face, leaving it the dead white color of ashes. He stared, fascinated, at Hedges's right hand that hung a few inches from his gun butt.

Hedges went on: "It wasn't flattering, what I heard."

"No, but it was true!" Pat blazed.

"Well, now, perhaps it was. By the way, Pat, do you realize the position in which this places the two of you? I can't let that story get around."

Tommy found his voice, and words came like babble from a delirium. "I won't tell! I won't. I swear it. Believe me . . . you have to believe me. I've always stuck with you. I've always played the game. . . ."

"Sorry, but the game of life is played with table stakes, and your string has run out."

Tommy's quick eyes shot to the door, to the window, and back to Hedges. Then they came to rest on Pat's Derringer that lay on the table. He started for it, but he didn't have a chance. Hedges's hand swung up from the holster.

The room rocked with explosion. There was powder smoke. The bullet drove Tommy to the wall. He hung there for a second, fingers clawing the logs, eyes glassy, then he fell against the table, and slipped limply to the floor.

Hedges watched without changing expression. He might have swatted a fly.

"You . . . murderer!" Pat gasped.

"Please. Isn't that a cruel designation for your fiancée?"

"I wouldn't marry you. . . ."

"No? Then I'll take you without the mumbling of some sky-pilot. You're mine. Do you hear me? Mine!" His voice lost its smoothness now. It was harsh; it filled the room like the pistol's crash had a moment before. "You're mine, just like this town of Bonanza Bar is mine . . . by right of conquest."

She was pale but defiant. "What do you intend to do?"

"There are only two things I can do . . . kill you, or carry you away until this whole unpleasant affair has blown over. As you realize, your testimony on behalf of the detective, Tarrant Andress, would be a little embarrassing to me."

"He has enough evidence against you to. . . ."

"But he'll do nothing with it. His string has run out, too. You see, I've decided not to wait on that bungling sheriff and the commissioner. Andress is in jail, and I've just sent four of my men over there to riddle him."

The impact of these words took the fight out of her. She was stunned, shattered. When Hedges seized her by the wrist, she went automatically, like a tired child. She rode away in the carriage, only dully conscious of its jogging passage over the rutted streets. Finally they stopped, and she allowed herself to be led through the side door of Hedges Enterprises.

Hedges shouted to the gray-haired cashier who was still on duty: "Open the strongbox and put those two leather satchels under the robe in my carriage!"

He watched while the old man opened the strongbox and staggered out with the heavy bags. Then he led Pat up the stairs to his office. He made a spark on tinder and lit the lamp. Next he went methodically through the drawers of his desk, destroying papers. This took about three minutes. One letter caused him to pause and smile—the gloating smile of a victor.

"See this letter, my dear? It's from Uncle Ramford. It was delivered by Tarrant Andress, remember?"

A *rattle* of hoofs on the street outside caused him to lay down the letter and listen. Feet *clomped* up the stairway. A familiar something about those steps knifed through Pat's apathy.

"Terry!" she screamed.

Hedges smiled grimly. He flipped out a gun, cocked it, waited.

"No!" Pat dived for the pistol, but Hedges pivoted to avoid her. The door was hurled open. Terry stood there, gun in hand. But Pat and Hedges were struggling so he dared not shoot. Hedges flung her aside and fired, but the bullet only sent splinters buzzing from the door. He cursed, turned on Pat, and swung a backhand blow that sent her spinning limply to the floor.

At the same second, Terry charged. Hedges had no time to bring his gun to play. The rush carried him against his desk.

There he pushed himself free, tried to shoot. Terry smashed the gun from his hand. Hedges cursed. He set himself and let go a smashing right. It landed like a sledge. Terry reeled, went to his knees, fell forward in a blind clinch.

They rocked across the room. Hedges at last tore himself free. He went for his left-hand gun, but the hammer tangled in his clothing. He tried to jerk it free. But Terry had recovered himself. He stepped in with a looping right hand that made Hedges stagger blindly. A chair tangled his feet. It toppled and crashed beneath him.

Hedges lay on his back, apparently stunned, but when Terry leaped in for the supposed advantage, both his feet drove up, catching Terry in the middle, doubling him, paralyzing him. Hedges was up, agile as a bobcat. He grabbed a leg of the chair and swung it.

Terry reeled and took a glancing blow. He toppled forward, arms finding the big man's waist. He sank to his knees, but he held on, fighting the black fog from his brain, fighting the creeping paralysis in his muscles. Hedges swung rights and lefts, but he had no chance for a solid blow. He tried to kick, but the arms tangled him.

Then, with a mighty effort, Terry stood. He stood, lifting Hedges with him. He lifted him higher and higher. He didn't realize what he was doing, or where he was going. All he knew was that life was flowing back through his body; that he had taken the worst Hedges could offer; that now the fight was his. He strode blindly with the big man held over his head—and then suddenly a gulf opened under his feet.

He was falling, falling like a man in a dream. He dully realized that he was at the bottom of the stairs, that he was standing and Hedges was on the floor. Hedges staggered up, faced him. It was then Terry heard Old Dad's voice right at his elbow.

"What?" Terry asked.

"I say, better let me finish this varmint off for good and all."

Old Dad stood in the door with both guns drawn.

"No," Terry muttered thickly. "This is my prisoner. I'm taking him to Salt Lake City . . . in irons."

He stepped forward, throwing his waning strength behind one last, smashing right. Hedges took the blow, reeled, and collapsed, bleeding and unconscious. Terry stared at him for a while, and started back up the stairs.

Pat was just coming from the office. With an hysterical cry she ran to him.

"Terry . . . I thought I'd never see you again . . . never."

Terry didn't know how long he stood there, but the sound of voices and *clomping* feet brought him back to reality. He listened. One voice boomed above the rest—Sheriff Gus Stiver.

"So you thought you could kill me, did you, Hedges? Waal, you ain't got me fooled no more. Commissioner Jonas told me how you was usin' the dignity of my office ag'in' that upstandin' detective, Terry Andress."

"Andress is a road agent!" Hedges shouted, conscious again. "A murderer!"

Terry hurried downstairs. Stiver was holding a gun on Lyon Hedges.

"Hello, Mister Andress," Stiver said with great deference. "Did you hear how this varmint's gang came over to the jail and tried to riddle me? But we're showin' 'em. Jonas has a posse together and he's caught a passel of 'em already. Arrested Shep, and the things he broke down and told about Hedges here makes amazin' listenin'." Stiver clamped a set of heavy manacles on Hedges's wrists. "Reckon I better take no chances with this bucko."

"You won't get away with this," Hedges hissed. He turned on Terry. "You'll go to prison. When Uncle Ramford hears how. . . ."

57

"Save it, Hedges." Terry looked at him with a reminiscent smile. "Try and see the humor of the situation. Remember how you said Uncle would pull down those spectacles and stare if I were to deliver you in irons?"

Dawn was streaking up over the mountains when Stiver bragged his last and led Hedges from the door. The crowd then quickly broke away. Terry looked for Old Dad. He was nowhere around. In fact, he hadn't been around for some time.

"Please, Mister Andress!" The little gray cashier pulled Terry by the sleeve. "I've been wondering about some gold. Mister Hedges had me put two satchels of gold under the robe on the floor of his carriage."

They hurried outside. The carriage was still there, but the robe lay flat on the floor, and nothing was beneath it except a folded scrap of paper. Terry opened it, and, by the light of dawn, read the words that had been bluntly scrawled with a pistol ball.

Jul. 18, 1864 A.D.
Rec'd with thanks—2 satchels g. dust as paymint in jail for services rendered as a detektif.

O.D.

Terry stood very still thinking it over. Then he smiled and slowly tore the note—tore it and kept tearing until it was a mass of tiny, crumpled bits of paper. He spread his fingers and watched the scraps catch the early light as they fluttered away in a hundred little zigzag courses.

If Jay Cooke was only my maternal gran'paw,

he hummed reminiscently, turning toward the door where Pat waited.

I'd have little Jenny Lind sing me to sleep. . . .

And, seeing Pat, he smiled: "Or would I?"

* * * * *

THE GAMBLER'S CODE

* * * * *

I

Shanghai Nivens, tall and slim, had one elbow propped on the deck rail as he looked down on the silt-yellow waters of the Yukon. Finally he turned and took notice of fat Senator Otman who was standing behind him.

"Cigar, Senator?"

"Ah . . . so." Senator Otman took the thin panatela, peeled off its star-decorated foil, and sniffed with the delicate anticipation of a connoisseur. "Excellent. You can't fool a Southern gentleman on the subject of tobacco, sir. Havana filler. No, not Havana, either. Vuelta Abajo. Where would a man find cigars of this quality in days like these?"

"I bought them in Seattle as you damned well know."

Shanghai Nivens struck a match and cupped it in his long, transparently white hands, protecting it from the northeast wind. He was considerably taller and younger than Senator Otman. His face was thin and dominated by a high-bridged nose, while the senator's was florid and blunt. He wore a close-clipped dark moustache. His mouth was rather broad, and he had a habit of barely revealing the tips of his even, bluish white teeth when he smiled. Despite the fact that Shanghai Nivens was dressed in Mackinaw and Scotch gray trousers, he looked considerably more fastidious than the senator in his cigar-ash-stained black serge.

The senator puffed a few times, letting fragrant smoke whip away on the raw, early summer wind.

"Financial trouble?" Nivens asked. He placed his cigar between his excellent teeth holding it there with delicate precision while drawing a lizard skin billfold from his inside pocket. "I warned you against these steamboat solo games. I suppose those Chechako sharpers have taken a quit-claim deed on our pants by this time."

"Indeed. Money was furthest from my mind. But now that the subject has chanced to come up. . . ."

Shanghai Nivens's face was perfectly composed, perfectly expressionless. He thumbed out a $10 bill, a yellow-backed gold certificate, and offered it with a dexterous movement holding it between fore and middle fingers. The senator pocketed it.

"Damn it, sir, this makes my mission more difficult than ever." The senator got it out in a single breath, then he paused from the effort and wheezed a few times. The early-summer breeze was sharp with a feel of the Arctic and melting snows, but despite that he felt obliged to remove his big, black Stetson and mop perspiration.

Shanghai Nivens waited, eyes intent on the senator's face. "Go ahead, Senator. Say whatever you planned. Or do you want me to say it for you. I'm a gambler. I carry a gun in my coattail pocket. There are two worlds . . . I live in one and Miss Crandall lives in the other."

"Damn it, sir, this is no joking matter. Look at yourself in a mirror. Judge for yourself what Miss Crandall sees. A handsome, personable man of the world. She wouldn't guess what you really are. A . . . a. . . ."

"Cad! Cad, sir, a cad!" Shanghai Nivens laughed and knocked a half inch of ash from his panatela. Despite his height and apparent slimness, he had an easy grace about his movements that hinted at an unexpected strength in his body.

"Very well, sir, if you will have it so, you are a cad. A man who has not earned a farthing through honest toil. . . ."

"What if Miss Crandall's in love with me?"

"Then she'll have to be given the opportunity of getting over it. I ask you, Shanghai, don't see her again. As your friend and companion. . . ."

"I'll jump overboard. But not right now. After supper." He laid a hand on the senator's shoulder, a coaxing, persuasive movement. "You need a drink. A drink will help you see this thing more clearly."

"I'll not be wheedled out of this. If that young girl has really been foolish enough to fall in love with you. . . ."

Nivens made an exasperated gesture. "Damn it, how many times do I have to tell you? I'm through with cards. I'm no longer a gambler. I'm a banker. I'm sole owner of the First National Bank of Scratchgravel, Territory of Alaska. You saw it yourself in Joe Lestrup's will. I haven't shuffled a deck of cards since San Francisco. I plan to arrive in Scratchgravel a banker, I plan to live and work as a banker, and leave as a banker."

"Sir, you will be a cardsharp to the end of your days."

Shanghai might possibly have shot another man for those words, but coming from the senator it was different. His eyes merely narrowed, and his lips formed a line thinner than usual beneath his close-clipped moustache.

The senator went on: "Bank? Bank be damned! In two weeks you'll either lose it across the green cloth or be dealing chuck-a-luck through the teller's window."

Shanghai steered him inside. A wood stove was glowing in the low-ceilinged bar. Nivens stood with his back to the fire, getting the chill from his long body. The room was jammed with roughly dressed men bound for Scratchgravel, Ruby, or the Klondike. Several of them spoke, and he answered, making certain to call each by his name. Wherever he went, men were proud to be known by him. Shanghai Nivens had long ago given up wondering why. He had brandy and plain water, drinking it so slowly that scarcely half of it was gone when the senator had tossed down his third straight bourbon.

A China boy came in on thick-soled shoes banging a tin kettle for supper call.

The dining room was big, with a low ceiling supported by twenty gilt pillars. Smoke from the kitchen lay blue beneath the hanging kerosene lights, making it hard to see. Shanghai Nivens paused just inside the door, superior height allowing him to look over people's heads. In the far corner was a table covered with white linen instead of the brindle cloth in general use. Red-faced Captain MacPhee sat at the head of the table. At one side of the table were two women, wives of Dawson City residents. Sitting with her back to the door was the girl, Joan Crandall.

Shanghai crossed the room. The girl saw him. She was small, blonde, with deep brown eyes. The combination was arresting.

Nivens said: "I'm sorry I was late. The senator was lecturing me."

Captain MacPhee regarded him with a watery expression and got grudgingly to his feet. However, he made a point of not suggesting that Nivens sit with them. One of the women, a stern matron, wife of the Inspector of Mounted Police in Dawson, smiled unexpectedly and said: "Mister Nivens! I'm sure Miss Crandall would like to have you dine with us. And I'm sure I would, too!"

Captain MacPhee's face turned a deeper tomato color than before but he uttered no objection. Nivens thanked the woman, and looked down at Joan Crandall. Color had mounted a little in her cheeks, making her look more lovely than ever.

She nodded, and he took the chair beside her.

The inspector's wife went on: "You must forgive us, Mister Nivens. Imagine, the story going around that you were a gambler. And all the time you were a banker. A banker, mind you."

Shanghai laughed impersonally. "Quite ridiculous," he said. There were starched napkins on the table. He unfolded one halfway and spread it across the knees of his Scotch wool trousers.

"A bank in Scratchgravel?" MacPhee exploded.

"The First National Bank of Scratchgravel. We're small, of course, but perhaps we will grow with the country."

"You see?" cried in the inspector's wife triumphantly. "And ever since Saint Michael's we've made a point of not asking him to sit with us. Oh, you must overlook it, Mister Nivens."

By moonlight the Yukon seemed vast and shoreless with waves rolling in little whitecaps across miles of mud flat. Wind kept striking the boat's superstructure, swinging it around, and the pilot was barely able to keep it up the channel.

The girl paused in the sheltered niche of her stateroom door, a dark wool cape drawn around her shoulders. Shanghai Nivens looked down on her. The half light made her seem younger than she actually was. He'd have guessed her age as twenty-two, but at the moment she seemed more like eighteen.

She said: "Captain MacPhee keeps insisting you're a desperate character."

He laughed and said something about a man needing to be desperate before he set out for such a country.

"But you are a banker?"

"I own a bank. The First National Bank of Scratchgravel. I've never even seen it. It was left to me by an old friend who died on his way outside this spring. He thought he owed me something because one time I'd been instrumental in saving his life. So, if owning that bank makes me a banker, that's what I am. I've been a lot of things. A cowboy, a schoolmaster in a mining town, gambler, drifter. In Scratchgravel, I intend to buy gold at an honest commission and invest my profit in mining development. If the country amounts to something, I'll grow with it. Otherwise, I suppose I'll drift again. The senator gives me a week to lose the whole shebang over the green cloth. We'll see."

Generally Nivens spoke with impersonal cynicism, but there was a deep sincerity in his words tonight. Joan Crandall had taken hold of the doorknob to go inside, but she changed her mind, turned to face him. Her eyes, looking up in his, were deep as midnight. Wind caught her cape, wrapping it around her youthful body. For a dozen years Nivens had wandered from one frontier town to another, flush-moneyed or broke, pursued by his own itching heel, searching for something without knowing what. There'd always been beautiful women. Soft and voluptuous women, but with a glitter hard as knife steel down inside. After a while a man gets to forgetting that girls like Joan Crandall exist anywhere.

She'd moved so he could feel the pressure of her shoulder, and there was a willingness about her that was hard to resist, but he remembered his resolution and stepped back.

"I guess maybe the senator was right."

She started to answer, but he shook his head, reached beyond her and opened the door.

"Good night," he said.

She was a vague outline through the screen, watching as he turned and walked away, bent and holding his Stetson hat against the wind.

There was shelter on the larboard side. He stood looking across mud flat and the long, whitish lines of driftwood deposited by countless other seasons of high water on the Yukon. Remote and purple-white the moon picked up the saw-tooth McKinley range.

The senator found him there. "Indeed, my boy. Then you told her."

"I told her I was a gambler. But what difference did it make? A girl's willing to forgive anything when she's twenty-two."

II

June night was scarcely night at all at that far north latitude, and it was breakfast time with the sun up four hours when the steamboat *thudded* to rest against the new log pier where the flood-swollen Tanana came in. A small, two-decked sternwheeler dating to the old days of the Fort Cudahay traffic waited for the thirty-five or forty who had bought passage to the new gold diggings of Scratchgravel on the Tanana. Among the number were Joan Crandall, Shanghai Nivens, and Senator Otman.

The Tanana stayed in its banks better than the Yukon, giving a smaller but more regular channel for the pilot to follow. Low, treeless hills rose on each side, with here and there a gully head showing bird tracks of unmelted snow.

About noon next day the steamboat touched at a miserable cluster of log shacks where the Tanana stood at the head of the Susitna Trail, and the morning that followed placed them in the sprawling log and tent town of Scratchgravel.

Miners, boomers, and Indians crowded the dock, and other men hurried as fast as they could along the muddy, dog-trail streets.

"Oranges aboard?" a rangy, black-whiskered man shouted.

"Oranges aplenty!" the mate called back.

A good share of the crowd started forward, and the mate, evidently thinking they might raid the cargo, reached through the hatch and lifted out a double-barreled shotgun.

"Oranges aplenty, but they'll go for six dollars a dozen. Buy 'em from Lester Bohne."

The black-whiskered man grinned contemptuously at the

gun and stood with one thumb hooked in the French-Canuck sash that was used in place of a belt to hold up his muck-smeared pants.

"Don't try to run that sort of a wing-ding through me, you Chechako son. I'll take that smooth-bore away from you and. . . ."

He went on talking with a loud swagger, throwing in many strong-worded threats of the frontier. He'd obviously had a pint too much. Joan had been standing by the rail. She turned away, pretending not to hear. Her eyes came to rest on a powerful man of thirty or so who was striding across the crowded dock. He was dressed a good deal like all the rest in rough wool and high-cuts, but there was something about him that stamped him as different. He had strength, poise, purpose. His eyes were narrowed; his mouth was drawn to a perfectly straight line.

The black-whiskered drunk was still talking in a loud voice.

"Murray!" A clerk wearing black sleeve protectors grabbed him and spun him around. "There's a woman up there."

Murray stopped abruptly. His bleary eyes roved the deck and he saw Joan. He stopped, mouth sagging open. By that time the big man had forced his way through the crowd.

"Murray!"

Murray started to turn. He didn't see the fist coming. The big man smashed him with a perfectly timed punch. Murray's head snapped, shaking his black hat loose so it fell to the deck, rolled, plopped to the river. He went back, struck the deck, and remained in a sitting position, hands braced behind him. He was out, eyes staring. The big man jerked him to his feet and held him for a moment. Murray was still out, knees rubbery, head lolling to one side. With a contemptuous movement the man flung him away. Murray struck the mud-trodden dock logs and rolled as loosely as a fresh-killed beef. The big man didn't waste another glance. He strode on to the landing stage that had just banged down. Passengers stepped aside to let Joan go first.

He said: "My dear! I'm sorry this had to happen."

Joan Crandall stood at the top of the stage, looking at him in wide-eyed fascination. She started toward him, and had taken three or four steps when she remembered Shanghai Nivens who was behind, carrying her two suitcases.

"Your friend?" Nivens asked softly.

"Yes. Mister Bohne. Mister Lester Bohne."

"No more than a friend?"

His voice was pleasant and impersonal. Perhaps she didn't even hear the question. Everyone was watching her, and the resolution of it embarrassed her.

She met Lester Bohne's eyes. He waited, not a dozen feet away, smiling. He had a handsome face now that his anger was gone. Back of him a couple of men were helping Murray to his feet. Blood ran from the corner of Murray's mouth, matting his black whiskers.

It was hard to tell which man Joan was looking at the most as she moved down the plank, balancing herself against the boat's rocking movements. When she was close enough, Bohne took her hand.

"I never expected you'd have this sort of an introduction to the town. It's not the usual thing, Joan. Scratchgravel has lots of raw edges, as I wrote and told you, but men here know how to treat a decent woman." Bohne ended the subject abruptly. "Joan, stand down and let me look at you. You're prettier than ever!"

She paused at the bottom cleat, said some small thing to Bohne, and let her eyes rove the crowd, and beyond, over their heads, at the muddy Front Street of the town.

"You're looking for the eminent gentleman? Your dad stayed in the cutter rather than wade mud. His arthritis has been troubling him a little."

Nivens stayed a step or two behind, a suitcase in each hand. Joan turned, smiled at him a little nervously.

"I . . . forgot. This is Mister Nivens. Mister Nivens . . . Mister Bohne."

Bohne looked up and met Nivens's eyes. He moved uncomfortably, setting his legs a trifle wider, placing hands on hips. He didn't like to stand so far beneath a man while being introduced. Things like that seem important to some persons. Bohne deliberately waited while Nivens put down the suitcases and extended his hand before he made any move. Then, still taking his time, he walked around the girl and placed himself on an equal level before shaking.

His hand was powerful. He smiled a trifle. "Nivens? Not *Shanghai* Nivens! I've heard of you."

"Thanks."

"I don't know whether you should thank me or not."

Bohne was still smiling, but in appreciation of his remark rather than through any good fellowship. As for Nivens, he was tall and inscrutable as ever.

Bohne asked: "Here practicing your profession? I should think you'd find things more rich-blooded at Dawson." Then to Joan: "Mister Nivens is rather famous in his line, you know. Or did you know?"

"I've already told Miss Crandall I was once a gambler."

Bohne arched his brows. Muscles showed at the sides of his strong jaw, and anger was bringing color to his neck and the sides of his face. He still kept his voice polite: "Once?"

Joan said, eager to smooth over the breach: "Didn't you know? Mister Nivens is the new owner of your bank. The First National Bank."

"Well, Nivens. You are taking a hand in the development of the territory, aren't you? I heard that poor Joe Lestrup had died on his way outside but I didn't realize he'd disposed of his interests. Let me congratulate you. I'm sure you'll be just the man to make the First National pay out." There was no reason for it, but Bohne shook hands all over again. "You'll let me drive you there, of course." Bohne seemed to be all over his anger now. A pleased animation filled him. He practically beamed at Nivens, glowed with good fellowship. "I have a cutter waiting. It will be a lot better than wading this Scratchgravel muck in those gleaming boots of yours."

The crowd fell aside, giving them room. A cutter with a small black horse between its shafts stood just beyond the dock.

A thin, gray man was standing in the box, smiling as Joan Crandall ran the last few yards. The step was too far from dock to cutter. Bohne lifted her across the intervening distance. The gray man was Palmer Crandall, U.S. commissioner. Even in the excitement of greeting his daughter he seemed furtive.

"You haven't remarked about my horse," Bohne said cheerfully, taking his place beside Joan. "I'll wager it's the only horse between White River Divine and the Koyukuk."

The animal had trouble budging the overloaded cutter, but once started its runners moved easily enough through the street's muck.

They passed along Front Street, a line of shanty saloons with here and there a barbershop, Chinese eating house, or a dinky store. Standing atop a knoll was a large, two-story building of squared timbers topped by a sign reading: *Bohne and Company, Freight and General Outfitters.*

"Mister Nivens is a banker," Bohne said pleasantly, addressing Commissioner Crandall.

"Indeed?"

"Yes, Mister Nivens is the new proprietor of the First National. It was willed to him, I believe, by poor Joe Lestrup. Lestrup died on his way outside, you know."

Bohne turned the cutter along a side street and drew to a stop before a two-story plank and log building fronted by a high platform sidewalk and a canvas awning that had evidently been flapping itself to shreds since the autumn before.

"Here it is," Bohne said.

His voice was smooth, flavored with a note of satisfaction. His eyes were narrowed and laughing. He stood up in the cutter, bowing a little, gesturing with a wide fling of his arm.

"The First National Bank!" he announced.

There was a sign across the front of the building: *FIRST NATIONAL FARO BANK*

Shanghai Nivens looked at the sign for a considerable time. Any surprise he felt was not reflected on his face. He looked down at the girl. She didn't meet his eyes. Her hands clutched the sides of the cutter seat, and spots of anger rose in her cheeks.

Bohne said to her: "You see, my dear, Mister Nivens is a banker as he said. A faro banker. A common enough occupation here, I'm sorry to say." He looked around at Shanghai Nivens. "This is the place isn't it?"

"Why, yes, I suppose it is."

Joan asked: "You knew this all the time?"

"Of course not. I'm sorry."

He placed one hand on the cutter box and with easy grace vaulted to the platform sidewalk. He stood there, tall and composed, and lifted his hat. Bohne was grinning. The girl was about to say something, but Bohne cut her off with a burst of brassy laughter. He slapped the horse's rump with the reins and swung the cutter in a sharp turn toward Front Street.

Shanghai Nivens watched the cutter out of sight. He picked a bit of lint from his Mackinaw, straightened the hang of it on his shoulders, and walked inside.

The First National was almost deserted. It had the smell of spilled liquor and tobacco smoke shut up for too long. There was a huge, round stove in the middle of the room and a wood-box large as a grand piano beside it. Card tables stood around, but only one was in use and that by a derelict who was asleep with his head on crossed forearms. Beyond, in the gloomy depths, was a bar of sanded and stained spruce plank, and to the right, given a sort of privacy by some peeled posts, were the tiger games—faro, roulette, and twenty-one. None of them was in action. Four men stood at the bar. The bartender, a surly, massive young man with a red, pockmarked face, was watching him without enthusiasm.

Shanghai crossed the room and paused by the bar to light a cigar.

"Who's running the place?" he asked.

The pockmarked bartender let breath snort through his nostrils. "Who in hell do you think?"

"You?"

"You don't see anybody else here, do you?"

"You're fired."

He blinked like he'd been slapped across the face. "What?"

Shanghai Nivens puffed the panatela to light, blew out the match.

"I said you were fired."

The bartender let out a loud-mouthed guffaw. "Listen to that, now. The Chechako tells me I'm fired. D'you hear that, boys?" He stopped laughing and twisted his lips down giving his scarred face a look of truculent brutality. "And who in hell d'you think you are? The duke of San Francisco?"

"I'm the owner."

"Joe Lestrup never sold this dump. He died of the black cough on his way outside without sellin' to anybody. I never heard. . . ."

"He willed it to me, and I'm the owner. Now get out from behind that bar."

"Well, I'm blowed. I do think the sport means it. Get out from behind the bar, he says. Well by the bald-headed old hell, that's just what little Quiggie boy will do. Get out from behind the bar."

He ripped off a chunk of soiled flour sack that served as an apron and came out. Bowed legs and heavy stooped shoulders combined to give him a gorilla appearance. His right hand was doubled into a fist.

Nivens took the panatela from his teeth using his left hand.

"I'm Shanghai Nivens."

There was no way of telling whether he spoke through natural courtesy, or whether the words were a warning. The bartender continued on for three steps. Then he stopped.

"Oh," he said. He licked his lips. His little, swine eyes were on Nivens's right hand that hung perfectly relaxed, its back toward him, a big, sky-blue diamond on his fourth finger catching the faded light. "Oh, well, why didn't you say so when you came in? I thought you was some smart Chechako givin' me a line."

He turned and started back around the bar.

"I said you were fired."

The bartender hesitated and thought it over. Instead of going behind the bar, he walked to a rear room and reappeared carrying a Mackinaw and Scotch cap.

"I got money comin'."

"Get it."

The man simply stood there. It seemed to take two or three seconds for anything to register on his brain.

"Go to the cash drawer and take it." When he didn't move: "Or isn't there anything in the cash drawer?"

"I been makin' change out of my pocket."

"Get out."

The bartender didn't say any more. He headed through the front door.

Nivens went behind the bar, glanced in the storage space beneath. He lifted out several bottles. The worst kind of hoochinoo. Finally he located a bottle of Hennessy brandy. A cork had been driven far down in its neck. He swung the bottle, breaking the neck cleanly with a single blow across the metal wash compartment. He flourished it, showing the tips of his teeth in a smile.

"My compliments, gentlemen. Compliments of the First National Bank!"

III

The upstairs had been intended for a hotel, but only one room had been completed. It was furnished with an iron bed, a table of whipsawed plank, and a couple of woven-willow chairs. After an almost continuous forty-eight hours without sleep, Shanghai Nivens was stretched out on the bed, fully clothed, breathing deeply.

Someone rapped at the door. Nivens sat up. He lifted a pearl-handled gun from between mattress and springs, slid it in a tooled-leather holster hung beneath the arm of his coat. He put the coat on.

"Who is it?

"Otman."

"Just a moment." He poured water from a brass pitcher, washed and dried his fingers, combed his hair, and opened the door.

The senator was still wheezing. "Damn this altitude." He stood for a while with the smell of soap and mop water flooding in from downstairs where a crew of Chinese were at work. He walked on to the table, lifted the brandy bottle. Empty. He banged it down. "Trouble. Sufficient unto the day. That bartender, Quig Haugen, he claims he had some special deal with Joe Lestrup about this place which I do not doubt he did. But verbal, praise be to God. As a disbarred lawyer, I tell you a verbal agreement is not worth the breath it was uttered with barring a predisposed jury."

"To hell with him."

"Indeed. So be it. But let us go on to a higher theme. To wit . . . that big-fisted Lester Bohne. He's made the point that a bank cannot be operated without the proper charter, and you have none."

"Frontier conditions, Senator. Have a cigar."

"Judge Crandall will issue a restraining order, and. . . ."

"And he'll wait till next summer getting a deputy U.S. marshal up here to serve it. If I accept and transport gold at a lower rate than Bohne, the camp will be on my side. So to hell with Bohne, too."

The senator snorted cigar smoke from his nostrils. "You hate him because he made a fool of you in front of that girl. It's not good business that's. . . ."

"I came here to operate a bank."

"But Bohne runs the town. He snaps the whip. . . ."

"He hadn't better snap his whip too hard or he'll end up with a mouthful of hobnails. These frontier camps are like that. They don't sell him their gold because they like him, or because they want to. It happens he's the only one with a way of hauling it out. It's either sell to Bohne or spend the better part of a year taking it outside yourself. And for that small service he takes just about half. Twenty-five percent impurity discount, and this Scratchgravel gold runs nine hundred fine. Ten percent insurance. Twelve and a half discount, and another five for transportation. Give me a straight, honest five percent and I'll reinvest in mining development and make a million."

"And what will Bohne be doing while you're making your

million, sir?"

"That's up to him. . . ."

"Up to him . . . and Colin Starr."

Nivens looked down on the senator for a while. "Colin Starr is dead"

"Colin Starr is alive, in Scratchgravel, living under the name of Barnes. Furthermore, he's Bohne's bodyguard. I saw him just this evening. He's grown older and he looks as though he'd ridden a few dry trails, but he's the same Old Bushwack, all right."

"Is he coming around to see me?"

"I wouldn't know."

"There's something else bothering you, Senator. What are you holding back?"

"Eh?" The senator jerked his head with an abruptness that dislodged ash from his cigar. "I sometimes think those stories about you reading minds are true."

Shanghai smiled.

"All right, but hold your temper. Joe Lestrup didn't die of pneumonia, or the black cough. It was aggravated by some broken ribs. Maybe a nicked lung."

"Bohne?"

"I believe so. Joe was fixing to buy gold here. Like you."

"In other words, Bohne got Joe down and kicked his ribs in."

The senator was perspiring. "Now, there's no use of you losing your head over this thing. No use walking into the lion's mouth. What's done is done. This is a rough country. Lestrup knew what he was up against."

"Lestrup was fifty years old. He weighed less than a hundred and forty pounds, and he never carried a gun in his life."

"It might have been an accident."

"No use of talking any more about it, Senator."

They went downstairs. The Chinese crew had finished scrubbing the floor and had started on the walls. A couple of French-Canuck axe-men were squaring the sill logs for a crib-work strongbox. At the bar a man was pyramiding glasses, stacking out bottled hoochinoo, getting ready to move it out. There were a couple dozen spectators.

The sun was setting, its last rays giving a delicate peach color to the weather-drab buildings of the side street. It struck the new banner hung across the First National. Nivens stood at the edge of the sidewalk, reading it:

FIRST NATIONAL BANK
OF SCRATCHGRAVEL
Our Seattle Depository—Puget Sound Savings & Trust
Gold Discount 6%, Trans. & Insurance 4%
Seattle Bank Certificate of Deposit Delivered Here Within 3
Months

The sign seemed to satisfy him. He had supper at a Chinese beanery and returned to the First National where work was progressing by candlelight. He was barely upstairs when a Chinese boy came to tell him of a visitor.

"Tall man?"

"No. Little Chechako."

"Send him up."

The Chechako was a mousy-looking man of forty dressed in a tweed business suit that looked misfit in that camp of Mackinaws and mukluks. He stood for a moment, looking at Nivens across the candlelit room, then, when Nivens nodded him inside, he seated himself stiffly on the extreme edge of a willow-wove chair, both hands on a leather portfolio. He cleared his throat.

"I'm Rimmel. Phillip Rimmel. Mister Bohne sent me. I'm his chief clerk."

Nivens offered him a foil-wrapped cigar. Rimmel took it,

tucked it in his breast pocket. He cleared his throat all over again,

"I'm here on a matter of business. Mister Bohne has entrusted me with a sum of money. That is, with. . . ."

"You mean he wants to deposit money in the First National? I'm sorry, but. . . ."

"Ah, no. You don't understand. Mister Bohne is willing to purchase your . . . ah . . . bank."

"Is it for sale?"

Rimmel smiled. "There is a saying. Something in a French novel. This novelist . . . he said everything on earth is for sale. Yes, that's what he said. Everything on earth."

"Alexandre Dumas added a phrase to that . . . provided, he said, the offer is big enough."

"Why, yes. I think he did say that, too." He fumbled with the portmanteau. "My employer has been very generous."

"How much?"

"One thousand ounces. Scratchgravel gold. That is roughly equivalent to fifteen thousand dollars. The gold to be . . . all delivered in Seattle."

"That was nice of you, Rimmel. The way you said it. It is to be delivered to me in Seattle. Better than telling me I'd have to get out of the country. You don't very often find that kind of courtesy in a raw camp like this. How did a man like you ever happen to come here, anyway? Abscond with the firm's money?"

Rimmel's fingers jumped so he almost dropped the portmanteau. His eyes were like a trapped coyote's. Nivens kept watching with his old, impersonal smile.

Rimmel tried to answer, but his Adam's apple seemed to be giving him trouble.

Nivens asked: "Is Colin Starr outside? Someone said you always worked as a team. Reward or punishment, all in one neat package."

"Colin Starr?"

"Call him John Barnes, then. Men like Colin accumulate lots of names."

Shanghai watched the little man's eyes. He laughed—a soft, easy sound, knowing he'd guessed correctly. No man can be a truly good card player without being able to judge the other man's excitement and learn things from it—whether he has the once in a thousand four-of-a-kind or whether he's making the big bluff of his life.

"Go down and tell your man I'd like to see him."

Rimmel was glad to get away. Nivens went to the bar for the last bottle of Hennessey, carried it to his room.

He drew the cork. A knock sounded. The door was unlocked, and the force of the knock swung it open. A middle-statured man stood in the opening, watching with eyes as gray and cold as knife steel.

"Hello, Colin. It's been a long time."

Colin Starr had a high-boned face with a complexion at once weathered and grayish.

"Why, hello, Nivens," Starr drawled. "I'm sure pleased to see you."

They shook hands. Nivens slid over the bottle and glass, waited for Starr, poured one himself.

"Here's to old times." They drank. Nivens put down his glass, dried his lips on a folded linen handkerchief. "I hear you're working for Lester Bohne."

"Yes, I'm working for Bohne. He treats me honestly. When you're working for a man, old friendships don't mean a hell of a lot."

Nivens nodded. The warning was about as plain as Starr could make it. "That's what I thought. People don't often change."

Starr gave these words a lengthy consideration. He sifted a

wheat straw paper full of Durham, twisted it, and licked it to shape, lit it over the candle flame. Then he said: "You're talking about Mossberg, aren't you?"

"Among others."

"It wasn't me who ambushed Mossberg on that Carbonate dump, even if those hammer-headed law dogs did wolf me out of Leadville because of it." His voice became frigid and deadly. "Maybe you don't believe that, Nivens. Maybe. . . ."

"If I tangle with you, it won't be about a man who's been dead for eight years. It'll be over something here, now, in Scratchgravel."

"What did you want of me?"

"Just a drink for old times. You went to Bisbee after Leadville, didn't you?"

"I killed a man in Bisbee."

"Then Del Rey."

"I killed a man there, too. I was guard for Nedros. After that I went to Butte City, and I killed a man there. Down in the Clipper Shades." He spoke with a bitter twist of his lips, after the manner of one deliberately torturing himself.

"Same old routine."

"People with property hired me to protect it. I did my job. If it hadn't been me, then they'd have hired somebody else. When it came time for someone to take the blame, I did that, too. I've been riding down the long coulée for fifteen years. After you get enough sheriffs on your tail, a couple more don't make much difference."

"Where're you going after you leave here?"

"What makes you think I'll have to leave?"

"You just got through telling me, Colin. If I put up a battle, it will come to a showdown, and in the showdown you'll have to kill me. You didn't say so in that many words, but that's what you meant."

"I won't have to kill you. Sure, you turned down the offer that Rimmel just carried in. You turned it down because you know Bohne's good for twice as much. But when it comes time, you'll move. I won't have to kill you."

Starr poured another drink, tossed it down. "That brandy's good after all the rotgut I've put up with this last year." He walked to the door, opened it. "I better go. They might think we were cooking medicine."

Nivens let him get two-thirds of the distance down, and started to follow.

"Barnes!" he called, using Starr's current alias.

Colin Starr turned. Nivens went on in a voice that could be heard in the street,

"If you have shooting on your mind, I guess tonight's as good as any time."

Everyone in the big room stopped what he was doing to watch. There were men standing around the front sidewalk, and they listened, too.

"Don't be a fool." Starr looked around noticing the silence that hung in the room. "You wouldn't have a chance of getting that gun of yours from its shoulder grab."

Nivens moved down slowly, step after step, watching Starr's eyes. The man was deadly with a gun, but the chances were he was under Bohne's orders to cause no trouble in public.

Nivens asked: "You wouldn't be a little worried about that?"

"I haven't even got a gun." Starr looked around. One of the Canuck axe-men was grinning. It brought him up like the point of a knife. His face looked more gray and predatory than ever with lines setting deeply at the sides of his mouth. He jerked his Mackinaw open, showing the absence of gun and cartridge belt. "I thought you might want to get a bullet through your eyes, Nivens, so I didn't take the chance."

Nivens paused halfway down the stairs. The entire room was

beneath him—spectators, Chinese mop crew, the bartender with bottles and glassware tacked out on the bar. He laughed and swung himself around. It was apparently a careless movement, pointless, yet silvered gun metal gleamed in his hand. No one watching him could say they'd actually seen him draw the gun, and yet there it was. He aimed waist high, pulled the double-action trigger. The gun pounded, sending a pencil of flame across the candlelit room. One of the bottles disintegrated, liquor spattering the wall. Again. Again. Two more bottles broke, and a fourth was shattered by flying fragments.

He turned, gun tilted toward the ceiling, a little wisp of smoke stringing from its muzzle. "You see? I can take care of myself all right. I wouldn't want you to feel sorry for me when you go gunning."

Starr let a laugh jerk his shoulders. "The same old Nivens. Always making the big play. You've lasted pretty well, Nivens. Maybe that's because you knew enough to do your shooting at bottles. I never tried to hit bottles myself."

He walked outside. The senator crawled from beneath a roulette table.

"That was a gaudy trick."

"Well, I'm by way of being a flamboyant guy." Shanghai reloaded the .32 revolver and thrust it back in the shoulder grab. "If Lester Bohne sends a gunman to visit me, I want people to know about it. If I'm shot in the back, I want them to know who to suspect. Maybe, if enough people know who to suspect, I won't be shot in the back."

IV

One of the big mines of Scratchgravel Gulch was McVey's Golconda. Unlike many operators, McVey believed in frequent clean-ups, and so he was the first who brought heavy moosehide pokes of color to the First National for deposit and shipment. There was suspicion of the new bank, and perhaps McVey shared it, but the vast saving promised by its more moderate discount overweighed it, and other big shippers followed him.

Bohne made no move to lower his discount and transportation charge in the face of competition, and a story made the rounds saying Bohne would refuse to transport First National gold on his steamboat. Asked the question pointblank by Malemute George Tyler, Bohne was evasive.

"Nivens never asked me. Maybe he intends to carry it outside on his back."

On the 14th of July, Pierre Roche, a French-Canuck in the employ of the First National was observed to go downriver in his birch *bateau,* and there was some joking that Pierre had the job of hauling gold all the way to St. Michael. The purpose of his journeys became apparent on the 28th when a steam launch of the Yukon Transportation Company arrived with Pierre and his birch *bateau* upended on the deck. The steam launch took aboard the contents of the First National's vault and departed. According to the bank's standard agreement, deposit slips on the Puget Sound Savings and Trust would arrive within ninety days.

The night of the steam launch's arrival and departure, Marshal Tim McSloy strode into the candlelit First National. McSloy was six feet one, with bulging shoulders and a battered-down nose. He paused for a while, looking around the room. The bar had been moved out. A waist-high rail divided the room in half. Behind it sat a Chinese manipulating an abacus with quick finger movements. At one side of the room stood the receiving cage with Clic Pope, a young, rather chinless man sitting by some big balances.

"Where's Nivens?" McSloy asked.

"I don't know," Pope answered.

"When'll he be back?"

"I don't know that, either."

"You don't know much, do you?"

Pope didn't say anything.

"Well, send for him."

"Who'll take care of the cage?"

McSloy laughed and spit on the floor. He pulled his Mackinaw apart and hooked thumbs in the armholes of his vest. The vest was cream-colored silk decorated with brown horseshoes, slightly soiled but still conspicuous. A badge was pinned to the vest, and a .45-caliber Colt sagged a plain belt around his waist.

"Nobody needs to take care of your cage. Beginning tonight this dump is all through."

"What do you mean?"

"Go get Nivens!"

Pope hesitated. Finally he opened the door and stepped out of the cage. He killed time by removing his sleeve protectors. The Chinese had ceased working his abacus and was peering over his glasses.

"Take care of the cage, Sing."

"No y'don't," McSloy brayed. "You stay where y'are, Chinaman! If there's anything I can't stand, it's a dirty, slant-eyed, cat-eatin' chink takin' a white man's job."

The senator had walked to the head of the stairs. He called down: "Your opinion hasn't much bearing on the matter, has it?"

McSloy spun around, watched with narrowed eyes as the senator came down looking bleary and rumpled from sleep. A smug, sneering smile spread over McSloy's heavy face. He rolled his chew of cut plug and squirted a thin stream of tobacco juice over the rail. "Well, if it ain't the senator! Been sleepin' off a jag?"

"Sir, if it was your intention to come here and insult. . . ."

"Git off your horses, Senator. We all know you. You're just a drunken stiff that Nivens carries with him for laughs. Banker be damned! Hearin' you call yourself a banker makes me want to throw up my supper. You and your Chinaman help!" He laughed again. "Well, you're all through. You and the bank both." He patted his pocket. "I got me an order here that says so."

"Let me see it."

"Go to hell. I don't do business with the help."

He walked to the gate leading through the rail and booted it open. "Sir, don't go in there!"

The senator was striding to stop him. His face, usually red, had turned purplish from anger. McSloy turned. He did it slowly, eyes narrowed until they were almost closed. "So you say I can't go in there."

The senator stood his ground. "Sir, it may be that you have a tin star on your vest, which you got by kissing the hindquarters of Lester Bohne, but. . . ."

McSloy drove the heel of his right hand to the senator's cheek. It struck with a force that snapped his head to one side and drove him to the floor.

The senator started to pick himself up. McSloy waited. He was grinning.

The outside door opened. McSloy spun around. When he saw it was Shanghai Nivens, the smile left his lips.

Nivens crossed the room and looked down on the senator. Then he turned to McSloy. "You knocked him down?"

McSloy swaggered a little.

"Did you?" Nivens repeated.

"You don't see nobody else around here that could've done it, do you? It'll teach the tub o' lard to shut up his gab. I come here on a piece o' duty and I'll not have some drunken whiskey stiff. . . ."

"What piece of duty?"

The senator made it to his feet. He fingered hair from his

eyes. "Indeed, sir, that hired hoodlum who calls himself a. . . ."

"Never mind," Nivens said in his old velvet voice. "Go ahead, McSloy. What piece of duty?"

"I got a paper here the U.S. commissioner empowered me to serve. Being duly appointed representative of the. . . ."

"Give it here."

McSloy drew out a folded document in duplicate. From the left pocket of his Mackinaw protruded the handle of a tack hammer, so he evidently intended to post one of them. Inadvertently, however, he'd handed both copies to Nivens.

Nivens unfolded them, compared them, scanned rapidly to the signature. He smiled.

"So you think those will close me up! Orders like this are outside a U.S. commissioner's domain. He's only a glorified justice of the peace."

"Those are legal papers, and. . . ."

McSloy stopped, staring as Nivens tore them down the middle, placed the halves together, and tore them again.

McSloy lunged forward, trying to grab them away. Nivens retreated a step, tearing the papers once more. He flipped them, the pieces striking McSloy's chest and fluttering to the floor.

"Get out," said Nivens.

McSloy's Mackinaw hung open. His hand came to rest near the buckle of his gun belt.

"Get out," Nivens repeated, his voice like sharp steel.

"It ain't me that's gettin' out," McSloy muttered. "You're all through here, tinhorn. You make a play for that tin pistol in your. . . ."

Nivens swung a short left to his mouth. The blow struck a trifle high on McSloy's chin and mashed teeth through his lower lip. He started to retreat, changed his mind, swung a haymaker right. Nivens let it miss, and the blow carried McSloy over the balls of his feet. He staggered to catch himself. Nivens set his heels and smashed a right that left McSloy stunned on rubbery knees. He reeled back, fighting for balance. His heel caught and he went down. His head snapped back and struck the floor.

His glazed eyes roved for a while after he'd thrust himself to a sitting position. They came to rest on Shanghai Nivens who was standing over him. His hand fumbled for the butt of his revolver. The holster was pinched under one hip. He had to jerk a couple of times to free the gun. Nivens waited for it to clear the holster, then his boot toe connected, not hard but with excellent precision, striking the "crazy bone" nerve center of his elbow.

McSloy's hand was paralyzed. The gun lay in bent fingers, muzzle resting on one thigh. He had no strength to clutch or cock it. Nivens plucked it with a careless movement, half cocked the hammer, spun the cylinder, and punched out the loads. There was even one in the suicide chamber beneath the hammer. McSloy had come expecting trouble. He tossed the gun back in McSloy's lap. "Get up."

McSloy made it to his feet. No swagger left now, only a blank, stunned sort of fear on his face.

"Get out."

McSloy lurched to the door, got it open, paused for a moment to look over his shoulder at Nivens. He staggered on, ramming against two men who had hurried from across the street to watch the excitement.

McSloy cursed, wheeled, swung a backhand blow that sent one of the men to the edge of the sidewalk, then he lumbered away.

"He'll cause you more trouble," said the senator.

"Not McSloy. He's had his belly full." Nivens took time to wrap a handkerchief around the bleeding knuckles of his right hand. "I don't mind so much having Bohne try to close me, but he could at least pay me the courtesy of sending his best gun hawk."

From his room upstairs in the First National, Shanghai Nivens could look over the dirt and tarpaper roofs of Scratchgravel and see the new house of massive spruce logs that had been finished for the U.S. commissioner and his daughter. Occasionally he would get a glimpse of the girl when she appeared briefly at the door or window, or he would watch her when she went riding with Lester Bohne in the bright yellow sulky he'd brought in on his steamboat. However, save for a single momentary meeting on Front Street, he had not been close enough to speak to her since his arrival.

It was late in August, three weeks after Marshal Tim McSloy had been driven from the First National. The steam launch had called for a third time, taken gold aboard, and left. Shanghai Nivens stood on the dock, watching the launch's furnace doors glow yellow in the early darkness, and disappear around the downriver bluffs.

There was a chill in the air. It had been freezing during the early morning hours, each day a little harder. The short, northern summer had about run its course. He tossed away his cigar, turned up the collar of his Mackinaw against the breeze from across the river. Torches were burning along the wide bottom of the gulch, and uphill along the terraces of the low hillsides where placer mines were busy, struggling to harvest the final drifts of thawed muck before the big freeze.

He heard someone coming and turned around. Joan Crandall had walked up through the half darkness behind him.

She spoke in a rapid, embarrassed voice: "I saw you standing here. I wanted to tell you how sorry I was. About the other day."

"About that first day?" His voice was easy and laughing.

"Why, that's nothing to be sorry about. I'd told you I owned a bank, and obviously I'd lied. I don't blame you for being angry." He gestured to show the subject would be better forgotten. "I thought this was your hour for riding with Lester Bohne."

The color in her face deepened. "Why did you mention him?"

"I don't know. Lots of times I stand in my room over the First National and look at your house. I see Bohne drive up in that two-wheeled sulky of his and take you riding along our two miles of road. It just occurred to me that this was your usual hour."

"I didn't know . . . that you . . . watched. I. . . ." She stopped.

"What did you start out to say? That you had no idea that I'd be that interested?"

"Yes! That's what I was going to say."

"I'm very much interested in you."

"But you never came to visit me. Not even to say hello."

"I've been thinking a lot about you. And about me. What you are, and what I am. Do you remember what the senator said? Back aboard the steamboat? He said I'd be a cardsharp to the end of my days."

"You haven't played cards since you came to Scratchgravel!"

"You know that?"

"Yes!"

She stood with her back to the wind, facing him. He took hold of her arms. He looked down in her eyes. She let herself be drawn against him, then with a movement of cat-like quickness she twisted away. Her eyes shone with defensive fire.

"You have no right. . . ."

"I'm sorry. Of course I haven't." Nivens still watched her eyes. She wasn't afraid of him, but of herself. He asked: "Is it Bohne? Is he the one you're thinking about?"

She didn't answer. Her eyes were not meeting his. She was

rubbing the flesh of her left arm as though his grasp had bruised her.

"Is it?"

"What if it is?" She spoke sharply. Then she overcame her defensive anger and spoke in an easier voice: "I'm sorry. It was my fault. I should have told you about Mister Bohne that night aboard the boat."

"You're going to marry him?"

"Yes."

"When?"

"I'm not . . . quite certain."

"You don't love him."

"Don't be ridiculous! Why would I marry anyone I didn't love?"

Shanghai could have asked why she'd come hunting him out if the only one she thought of was Bohne. He didn't. Instead: "We're going to have a little struggle here, Bohne and myself. Business struggle I suppose you'd call it. It'll likely come along with the big fall clean-up at the mines. Wait until then before you marry him."

"Why?"

"I was in hopes something would make you change your mind. Bohne and I will prove what we really are in the showdown." He laughed with a mirthless jerk of his head. "Maybe you'll be glad enough it's Bohne and not me by that time. Or it could be the other way around."

"Don't fight him."

Her words startled him. "Why do you say that?"

"You haven't a chance. He has the law . . . everything. He'll make you a good offer. Why don't you . . . ?"

"Well, I'm damned!" He laughed again, more bitterly than before. "Is that why you came here? To ask me to back out?"

"It isn't what you think! It isn't because I want one side or the other to get this gold discount business. It's not for Lester. It's just that I can see what's coming. Killing, perhaps. Father says so. You challenged his authority. Father's authority. If he lets one man get away with it, he'll have to let everyone. Pack your things and go outside . . . that's what he says. He can't let you stay. Next time it won't be a coward like McSloy. You can't go on, taking the law in your own hands. . . ."

"Bohne can't, either."

"But he hasn't done anything to. . . ."

"He's taken a very firm grip on the law, hasn't he?"

Joan saw what he meant—the subtle dig at her father being owned by Lester Bohne. "My father is honest! You know yourself you've been operating your bank without any authority, with no franchise, or charter, or whatever. . . ."

He lifted his eyebrows.

"Don't laugh at me!" she fairly screamed.

"I'm not. I was wondering how you knew I didn't have a charter. Or how your father, the commissioner, knew. He sent McSloy around to close me up without even bothering to ask."

She was ready to make a sharp retort. She stopped abruptly and turned, peering toward Front Street. Wheels rattled on the rough roadway, and the sulky, with its small black horse, was outlined against sluice torches up the gulch.

Lester Bohne's voice: "Joan?"

They could hear his boots approaching. "I'm here!" Joan called.

He paused, peering through the dark. "Is someone with you?"

"Hello, Bohne," Nivens said.

"Oh. You." He walked on. Darkness covered his face until he was quite close. He'd had time to wipe any surprise and anger from it. "How are you, Nivens?" he asked civilly enough.

"Excellent."

"I see your steamer came. Was that your second shipment?"

"My third."

From his tone, Bohne might have been discussing the probability of frost that night. "You'll catch cold with no more wrap than that thin cape," he said to Joan.

"I was watching the boat. . . ."

"I had an idea you'd be here. They'll be waiting supper." He offered his arm. She took it. "I'll be seeing you," he said to Nivens.

Bohne had a way of saying things with apparent carelessness, putting the real meaning a little below the surface. On this occasion he did it subtly enough to bring a half admiring smile to Nivens's lips as he watched them drive away.

"Sure you will, Lester," he said softly. "And I'll be expecting you."

V

Wind rose that night, carrying the first snow of winter through the wide passes of the Brooks Range, across the rolling barrens, the Yukon and the Tanana to make little, foot-deep drifts along the sheltered sides of Scratchgravel's new-built houses. The snow stopped, leaving a grayish cold day.

Placer mines worked in a final fever of activity with muckers going eighteen and twenty hours at double pay, wheelbarrowing dirt along the plank runways to sluice head boxes. There was heavy freezing in the uplands to the south, and water fell to half its former volume. All but a handful of operators stopped moving muck and utilized the diminished flow to clean the riffles. The season's last, and biggest, clean-up was under way.

Johnny McVey stamped half-frozen mud from his boots on the First National's plank sidewalk and came through the door, staggering under the weight of a cowhide valise. He placed both feet widely, got hold of the handle with both hands, and lifted it to the cashier's shelf.

"You'll never get another boat downriver this season," he said. "You could get her down the Yukon, maybe, but not through the Bering Sea. There'll be floe ice in the pass so not the biggest fool skipper out of Seattle will put his rust-bucket boat through. Not even for gold cargo."

"Shanghai said we'd get the clean-up out," young Pope said with the air of one who's answered the same thing many, many times. He opened the valise and commenced lifting out its contents—gold in Siwash-tanned moose-hide sacks. Each sack, although scarcely larger than a man's two fists, contained between eighteen and twenty pounds of gold.

He opened the first and dumped it in the balance scale's pan.

"Nivens said to tell everybody that. Said we'd get it to Seattle this fall, and a certificate of deposit back as promised."

"How in . . . ?"

"I don't know, McVey." He commenced dropping weights and moving riders to bring the balance scale to equilibrium. "I don't know, and neither does Lester Bohne."

"I hear Bohne has finally lowered his discount rate to meet yours."

"That's what I hear." Pope lifted his hands and waited for McVey to agree on the weight. McVey nodded with a mere glance at the scale. "But Bohne's gold stays locked up here at Scratchgravel till Bering clears, and maybe that's next July. We're still getting the business."

"I'd still like to know how Nivens expects . . . oh, the hell with it. Nivens is foxy. I'm not worried. This is my fourth shipment this summer. I already got back cashier's slips on two of them. I can lose this one in the bottom of Norton Sound and still be money winner on the difference between First National rates and the robbery gouge that Bohne took."

As usual, McVey was ahead of the big rush. For a week afterward the First National handled a continual stream of gold.

Then, one cold morning, it diminished to a trickle.

Shanghai Nivens had been in the cashier's cage since noon. He relinquished his place to Pope and walked to the front window.

Outside darkness had settled. Only a scattering of torches now burned along the placer mines on Number One and Number Two benches, visible from the First National, but Scratchgravel itself made up for them with gambling and variety houses ablaze with light. Harvest was over and a time for celebrating was at hand. Standing there, in the front window, Shanghai could see the ceaseless stream of men that kept the batwing doors flapping at the Paradise House across the street.

The town had a strange feel to it. Boom towns get in a man's blood. They affected Nivens like some men are acted on by liquor. They seemed to lift his feet a little from the earth and carry him in a flood current of excitement, putting a giddiness in the pit of his stomach, making his hands long for the crisp riffle of pasteboard.

He jingled a couple of nuggets in his pocket, hesitated by the door. It was his worst time, as he knew it would be. Now with the fight about over, the harvest in, the First National a royal-flush success—cards are harder to quit than opium or whiskey.

A prospector from the Chena came in tracking snow from his mukluks. A heavy poke of dust was in his hand.

"It'll get to the States this winter?" he asked. "I got folks down there."

"We'll deliver it in Seattle inside a month."

"How?"

"It'll get there."

The prospector grinned. "If you say so, Shanghai." He winked. "Big game at the California Club. Draw. That's your game, ain't it? Draw and no limit. Ladue and McVey are both in it. I hear tell they put props under the table to keep the gold from bustin' her down. No place for a sourdough like me that ain't got a pot to make coffee in or a window to throw it out of." He winked again. "You goin' up yonder, Shanghai?"

Shanghai Nivens was glad he'd put it that way—straight out and loudly enough so everyone could hear. It made it easier to say no.

The senator had come down the stairs looking at him in a peculiar manner.

"What's wrong?" Nivens asked.

"You better go upstairs and see for yourself."

Nivens climbed the stairs. He'd had an office finished off adjoining his room. The office door was open. He stopped to peer in its deep shadow. He caught someone's movement and recognized it.

"Joan?"

"Yes."

He was struck by the familiar perfume of her hair, the sense of her nearness as she walked to the door.

She spoke in a voice tense and scarcely louder than a whisper: "I had to see you. I came in the back way." She was out of breath. She gestured to the senator who'd followed and was standing at the head of the stairs. "He won't tell?"

"You can trust the senator." He smiled a little and said in a soft voice: "You can trust him further than you can me."

She came close, so close he could sense the rapid throb of her heart.

She said: "I had to tell you. A United States marshal is coming. From Copper City or Wrangell . . . whatever that town is called down at the end of the Richardson Trail." She stopped. "Are you listening to me?"

"No."

"This is no time to joke. I said there was a. . . ."

"You said there was a U.S. marshal."

He drew her to him. For the moment she was surprised, yet passive in his arms. Her head was tilted up, her lips parted.

Then she jerked back. "Let me go!" she whispered furiously. "Let me go!"

He let her slip away.

"Don't make it any worse for me than it is," she said.

"All right. They're bringing in a United States marshal. What else?"

"Maybe he's in town now, but I don't think so. They didn't expect him before tomorrow noon. The steamboat was grounded on Deadman Bars, so they went for him in the canoe."

"This marshal, he intends to close me up?"

"Yes. You can't fight a United States marshal like you did McSloy."

"When the marshal comes, I'll do exactly what he tells me."

She hesitated for an instant, then she moved away. "I have to leave now. Father is home. He'll get to wondering."

"I'll walk part way."

A narrow, dark stairway led down to the alley door. There was scarcely room in it for Nivens and the girl to walk abreast. He paused after a few steps, sensing movement in the dark beneath him.

"Who is it?" Nivens called.

There was no answer. Just the sag of stair boards under someone's weight. The complaint of another stair. He was climbing toward them. Nivens knew who it was. It was Lester Bohne. He'd followed the girl.

"Bohne?" Nivens asked.

"Yes!"

Joan started forward in surprise. Nivens took her arm and with gentle pressure pushed her against the wall, held her there while he went down the next step alone.

No sound. Bohne had stopped.

"What do you want?" Nivens asked chiefly to get an answering sound and guess Bohne's distance away.

"I have nothing to say to you. Not right now. I came for Miss Crandall."

"I'm taking her home."

"Please!" She was behind Nivens, pulling at the shoulder of his Mackinaw coat. "I don't want any trouble."

"Go upstairs."

Bohne spoke: "I've taken quite a bit from you already, Nivens. I'm not going to take any more. Now get out of Miss Crandall's way." He waited for Nivens to make a move. Then his voice in a harsher whisper through his teeth: "You hear me? Get out of her way. I should kill you for taking my fiancée to your rooms."

"That's a lie, and you know it."

Bohne didn't answer. He was climbing—closer than Nivens thought. Nivens caught the impression of his shadow lunging forward and drove the heel of his boot in an instinctive movement of defense. It struck Bohne somewhere along his massive shoulder, the force of it turning him a quarter way around without stopping him.

His shoulder struck Nivens waist high, drove him back. Nivens almost fell, caught himself against the wall. He twisted to free himself, set his heels, tried to swing a blow to Bohne's jaw.

Bohne was too close. He took the fist short of it apex, rammed close, wrapping one arm around Nivens's waist.

Nivens tried to punch his way free. The narrow stairway was to Bohne's advantage. Nivens, tall and quick, needed room to maneuver. It was three or four steps to the top. He tried to back up, but Bohne's pressing strength made it impossible.

Bohne came around with a short right, bent his arm at the last instant, and his elbow struck with the impact of a sledge.

It paralyzed Nivens's neck and shoulder. Darkness rolled across his eyeballs. He knew he was falling, he seemed to be falling for many seconds, and he could do nothing about it.

Shanghai Nivens opened his eyes. Candlelight hurt them. "Where am I?"

"Indeed, sir, in your room." The senator was working over him with a cold towel.

"Where's Joan?"

"Gone with her fiancé. Now just lie still. You seem to have absorbed a beating."

Nivens lay back and closed his eyes. His face felt raw and hot as though he'd scrubbed the skin from it in falling down the stairs. The senator was applying something that smelled like witch hazel.

"You have, sir, accumulated numerous welts and lacerations which I don't doubt will be more painful to your pride than to the general state of your health. And well merited, sir. You have been looking for a pummeling ever since your first meeting with Bohne down on the docks."

"The hell with you," Nivens said.

He got up. His neck ached and he seemed to be going in a quarter circle as he crossed to look at himself in the mirror. His face was scratched along one side, but it looked better than it felt.

He changed clothes, combed his hair, rubbed dirt from his boots with a soiled handkerchief. Then he lighted a panatela and went downstairs.

Mist covered the front windowpanes. He wiped some away and looked out. Wind was coming in little gusts, swirling powdery snowflakes, forming little, shifting drifts in the back current caused by the First National's platform sidewalk.

He turned away. No customers. Even the Chinese bookkeeper

had nothing to do.

Nivens said: "We might as well close up for the night. There's a poke of company dust in the drawer. Divide it up. You've earned a celebration."

The wind blew snow intermittently through the night, keeping Scratchgravel's streets mostly deserted while celebrating ran high in her saloons and variety theaters. Nivens hunted out his crew of French-Canuck dog drivers and worked most of the night moving gold through the First National's rear door and loading it in canoes that transported it in repeated trips to Porthill, five miles upriver. Thence it would go by freight sled to the new town of Valdez at the end of the Richardson Trail. Nivens had made his preparations quietly, and no one suspected his intention of using this recently discovered route whose two hundred miles would short cut the three thousand miles of Yukon and ocean to place Scratchgravel within reach of winter boats from Seattle.

At Porthill the gold would await snow for sled runners.

It was 1:00 next afternoon when Nivens came downstairs at the First National.

He stood by the front window, looking out on the cold street. Only half an inch of snow had fallen, and the ground was still mostly bare. After half an hour he went out for breakfast. He returned a minute or so before a red-faced, soft-looking man of thirty entered with Palmer Crandall, the U.S. commissioner.

Crandall said something in a low voice, and the younger man took time to look around the place. Then, still without speaking, the stranger took off his fur mittens and unbuttoned his rat-skin coat. Nivens noticed that his fingers trembled a little.

"Nivens?" he asked.

"Yes. I'm Nivens."

The stranger fumbled with more buttons, opening his

corduroy suit coat. A badge was pinned on his vest. "I'm Carpenter. J.C. Carpenter, deputy United States marshal. I have an order signed by the commissioner."

Nivens took it from his hand and read carefully to the end.

"May I keep it?"

"Of course." It was evident that Carpenter had expected more trouble. "I'll have to . . ."—he hunted for the right word— "to impound the contents of your vault until the court decides one way or the other."

"All right. Go ahead. It's all yours. The responsibility for it, too. I'll be going outside to Seattle in a few days. I plan to start action in federal court. Keep everything just as you found it because I expect to be back." He turned and faced Crandall. The man looked thinner. He smelled of liquor. "Do you understand that, Commissioner?"

"You can't bluff me . . . you and your federal suit! I'm aware of my emergency powers here."

"In other words, you intend turning over the contents of my vault to Bohne and Company."

"I didn't say that."

Nivens laughed and gestured at the strongbox. "Go ahead, gentlemen. Impound and be damned." He stepped from the front door, then he thrust his head back inside. "Pope, have an inventory made. Carpenter and the judge will sign it."

VI

Somewhere a piano was playing, one of those mechanical, nickel-in-the-slot affairs with an assortment of banging cymbals and Swiss bells. Shanghai walked down Front Street to the California House.

He went through an arch to a semi-private gambling room in the rear, rapped at a closed door without getting an answer. He went inside. The room was an office belonging to the California's owner, Miller Loftus, but Loftus was not there. A short, ruddy-faced man was sleeping on the couch.

The man sat up, putting aside the rabbit-skin blanket that covered him.

"Dieu! Thees tam? Dark?" He was Putois Charley, a French-Canuck, one of the axe-men who had built the First National strongbox.

"Not dark yet, Charley. It's around two-thirty. You've been asleep about five hours."

"I feel like bear wake up in hollow tree. My back she's ache from carry gol', my hands bleed from canoe paddle. What you want now, hey?"

Nivens jerked his head in the direction of the First National. "I've just been closed down."

"Hah! The marshal. I lak feed heem to gray wolf, thees marshal."

"Hell will pop when they find out the gold is gone. Bohne will do anything including murder to stop us getting it outside. This is the big one. You paddle back to Porthill and tell Pierre he may have to move whether there's snow for his runners or not. Tell him that and come back. I'll meet you here." Nivens paused in the door. "Where's the canoe?"

"Down under dock. Canoe dock."

"All right, only don't let Adams see you from the wharf shanty."

There seemed to be a little more snow in the wind when he got outside. It would have to come a lot harder before it made sled going easy. Pierre Roche and his dog drivers could get by with a couple of inches if they had to. They'd be on gently rising ground toward the Gulkana. Snow would be deeper there, and across the pass to the new government trail up Copper River. Snow might give out on the other side, of course. It was still mostly rain and autumn fog near the Pacific, but he could get down the Copper by canoe and keep his appointment with the steamship, *Jacob Bearce,* at Valdez.

He walked back up the side street, watching the front door of the First National. No excitement. It would take them a while to find out he'd spent the night before moving the yellow metal leaving substitute sacks of black sand—the heavy magnetite and garnet that could be found heaped by every clean-up rocker in the gulch. He smiled a little, thinking that the substitution might never be noticed at all.

He entered the Paradise. Forty or fifty men were gathered at the bar and the gambling games. A woman was dealing a faro spread. Klondike Mary. Still young, but her painted face was lined and hard.

Klondike Mary drew two cards with deft movements of diamond-studded fingers. Then she sat back and lighted a brown-paper cigarette.

"There's Shanghai Nivens," she said for the room to hear. "The same Shanghai Nivens who laid fifteen thousand on a pair of jacks in a Butte City stud game, and now he wouldn't back Big Casino himself with grub money in a China house."

Nivens smiled faintly.

The crowd grinned and enjoyed it as Mary continued: "Good old Shanghai. I hear he's waiting for a frock coat and congress collar from outside so he can deck himself out like Rothschild in his glory to go uphill to Lester Bohne's wedding. How about that, Shanghai?"

"I haven't even been invited."

He was tall and unperturbed, standing now by the window, watching the street through a hole he'd dug in the frost. He smoked a cigar slowly. A man came from the First National. Judge Crandall, almost running in the direction of Lester Bohne's store. The gold had evidently been missed.

He turned away from the window, glanced at his watch. It

had been thirty-five minutes since he'd left the California. Putois Charley would be well on his way upriver.

He walked to a solo game and sat down beside Cal Ludlow, a professional gambler he'd known in Carson City.

"You can have this chair in a minute," Cal said. "I haven't had breakfast."

It was the first game Nivens had been in for over three months, and sitting there didn't mean he'd gone back to cards. It was merely a chair from which he could briefly glimpse the First National when the Paradise's front door opened and closed.

He lost steadily, playing too many short solos to kill his impatience. A Negro swamper came around to light extra candles as darkness settled outside.

"Snowing?" Nivens asked.

"No, sah. Not yet, Mist' Nivens. But it looks mighty like somethin'."

Nivens glanced at his watch. Two hours had passed. It was time for Bohne to be starting his play. Bohne wouldn't just stand around and weigh beans in that store of his when the big clean-up was slipping from his fingers. He'd fight for it—fight for the big commission of hauling it outside.

The crowd was growing larger. Someone was banging a honky-tonk piano. A sourdough with a snoot full of hooch came in, elbowed to the bar, said something. Nivens caught the sound of his own name. He shuffled chips, no change in his face. The sourdough repeated, and the bartender said something low to quiet him.

"I'll cash in now," Nivens said.

He took the credit slip and thrust it in his Mackinaw pocket, made his way through the crowd.

"What were you saying about me?" he asked the sourdough.

"Nothing. I didn't say a. . . ."

"It's all right. I'm not on the prowl." He bought the man a drink. "Now what was it?"

"Just that ruckus of McSloy's."

Nivens refilled the sourdough's glass. "What's McSloy up to?"

"Why, he's down at the Garter, last I saw. He claims you lit out with every damned dollar in the First National strongbox."

"So I'm an embezzler. And what does he want the boys to do with me?"

"Says they ought to give you the vigilante treatment."

"Have they sent for the rope?"

"Hell, Nivens, the boys ain't really believin' them things. Not yet. All they want is their gold back. They know it didn't go downriver on the steam launch because it didn't come through after clean-up."

"You say they're down at the Garter?"

"Yeah."

He went out with everyone watching him. The Garter gambling house stood at the lower end of Front Street.

Nivens stood on the sidewalk out front trying to see through the steamy windows. Overhead a banner was snapping in the wind. *Tuesday—the Black Pearl vs. Buzz Noonan—20 rounds*

Men came crowding through the front door, and none coming out. They weren't talking about a boxing match.

He went inside, paused in shadow to look across the room, through an arch to the dance hall. Usually an orchestra banged incessantly from mid-afternoon until the last gold-strewing customer was gone at night, but now there was no orchestra, no girls in flashy short dresses earning their brass percentage checks on the dance floor. Men filled the hall two-thirds to capacity. Someone was making a speech. Nivens climbed some stairs to the balcony, went inside a screened box that looked down on the stage and dance floor.

The speaker, surprisingly, did not have hanging on his mind.

"I don't think we ought to do a thing till the U.S. marshal comes and has his say!" he was shouting. "Who's seen the Chechako?"

"Set down, Clarkson!" somebody shouted. "Who are you to get your paddle in. You ain't got a thing in that bank."

Clarkson grumbled and edged back among the crowd. Marshal Tim McSloy leaped to a bench and shouted: "Damn it all, I already said a dozen times it ain't goin' to do no good to stand around here yawpin'! The gold's gone. It's stole. Thing to do is catch him before he jumps town. Pretty soon it'll be too late."

"Catch who?" It was McVey. He was working his way through the crowd. Evidently he'd just come in. His face was red from wind, and his rat-skin ear flaps were still down. "Who is it you want to catch?"

"That tinhorn that calls himself a banker."

"Nivens?"

"Of course, Nivens. Maybe you ain't heard about it, McVey. A U.S. marshal came and closed down that deadfall he called a bank. Nivens didn't have any more charter for a bank than I did. Opened the vault and know what they found? Black sand! Bags of it. And not more'n a dozen ounces of real dust in the place."

McVey laughed. "How much did you lose, Marshal?"

"Not a cent. I had brains enough to bank at Bohne and Company."

"With the man you work for. And now Bohne's sent you here to start a lynch party."

It was the truth, and McSloy's face showed it. He leaned forward, looking down from the bench at the smaller man. "No, Bohne didn't send me. I'm marshal here. . . ."

"Necktie parties are a hell of a thing for a marshal to be

heading." He laughed contemptuously. "You! Officer of the law!" McVey climbed the bench and waited until noise abated. "I got upwards of three thousand ounces of dust tied up in the First National. It's my fourth clean-up this year. The others got through all right, and I got cashier's slips from Seattle on two of 'em already. I could drop this whole shipment and still end up winner on the money I've saved by not banking with Bohne. But I don't expect to lose this shipment. I don't expect to lose a dollar. If Nivens hid the gold somewhere, I imagine you don't have to look very far for the reason."

A short, red-faced man bellowed: "Sure, it's all right for you to crow! You're already money ahead like you say, but how about us that only made one clean-up this year? Every single dollar I took out since the thaw was tied up in his vault. But it ain't there now. It's gone, and. . . ."

"Because he had to get it out of the way."

"He took it, didn't he? Signed a receipt for it. Now it's gone. I say catch him while we got time. I say a rope is good. . . ."

"Take it easy, Crawford," McVey warned.

"You take it as easy as you want to. You got plenty money. Catch him, I say, and make him dig up. *Dig up or swing up.*"

McVey was still trying to talk. Voices drowned him out. Men were pushing forward, moved by the aptness of Crawford's final words. Dig up or swing up. Somebody pushed McVey and he almost fell from the bench.

A big, raw-boned miner sprang to his place. "Sure. Catch him. Make him dig up or swing up. I come from Valdez, and they found out how to fix thieves down there. A stiff rope and a short drop. That's plenty good thief medicine."

"Git the senator, too," came a voice.

"Sure," brayed McSloy. "That big windbag's as bad as Nivens."

"Not now he ain't." It was the drunken sourdough for whom

Nivens had bought drinks. "I just been talkin' to him." He wanted to swagger a little and show his importance. "He just left the Paradise. I don't know where. . . ."

"You hooched-up fool!" McSloy sprang over, rammed through the crowd, collared the drunk, and dragged him off his feet. He shook him back and forth like a malemute would shake a poodle—shook him until his fur cap fell off and his greasy dark hair was strung over his face. "You told him what was goin' on down here, didn't you?"

"No, I didn't. Honest. Lemme go. I wouldn't do nothing like that. Tried to get him to stay there . . . till I could get down here."

McSloy flung him away. Exertion made him wheeze. A dozen men were trying to get a word in. One of the dance-hall girls screamed obscenities in a shrill voice.

Nivens had seen mobs before. He could judge the temper of this one. It was mounting toward action.

He slowly backed through the dirty damask drapes. The hall was deserted. He'd never been upstairs in the Slipper before, but those variety houses were always built about the same, the hall circling the boxes and thence to a side entrance provided for those who wanted to attend without being seen from the floor below.

The side door led to an alley, past the rear ventilator of a Chinese café with its damp grease-and-onion smell, and from there to a path that led among the slattern huts that had grown without plan around the business district. It was three or four hundred yards to the First National.

He crossed the street. Wind was carrying hard pellets of snow. It was getting colder. He stepped to the platform sidewalk and tried to see inside, but the First National's windows were too thickly covered by frost.

He walked to the rear entrance, stepped inside. Narrow stairs in darkness—no sound. Only a distant *creak, creak* of the high-wired stovepipe giving with the wind.

He climbed the stairs. His office was chilly with the wood fire gone out. He lighted a candle, looked around for clothes, put on an extra wool shirt, stuffed wool socks in a pocket of his parka, dropped the parka over his arm.

He went to the front stairs, looked down. Carpenter, the U.S. marshal, stood with his back to the stairs, peering through a hole dug through window frost.

God, he mused, *must be sixty of 'em.*

Nivens heard their voices then. He smiled a trifle, wondering what this United States marshal would do with a lynch party on his hands. Look for cover, probably.

He took a step toward the rear stairs. Voices from that direction, too. They'd surrounded the place. Someone must have seen him crossing from the Paradise.

There were still ways of getting out—through the fire hole to the roof, down to the one-story barbershop next door. Or he could simply drop from the window of his room. Either way would be simple enough.

The front door was flung open and men were stamping in. He recognized McSloy's voice. It was the sound of McSloy more than anything that changed his mind. A man can lay plans, but he never knows just how he'll act when the blue chips are in the pot.

Nivens walked down the front stairs. Men were crowding in. He was halfway down the stairs before anybody noticed,

"There he is!" He recognized the voice of Quig Haugen, the pockmarked bartender he'd had trouble with that first day.

"What do you want?"

Nivens's voice was loud, but it had a knife-steel quality that cut through the mob, stopping them where they were.

Haugen had a length of plaited babiche rope in his hands,

and he kept twisting it around his bent forearm as he looked up at Nivens. Some of the others carried guns strapped in sight. There was one man with a double-barreled shotgun.

Three or four seconds passed, although the tension made it seem longer. It was McSloy who finally came forward. "Dig up that gold, Nivens."

"What is this, a robbery?"

McSloy laughed from the side of his loose mouth. "Robbery? You hear that? He talks about robbery!" Somebody in the open door laughed, and the sound of it helped build McSloy's confidence. "Listen, tinhorn, I'll give you just exactly ten seconds to git that gold."

"The gold happens to be on its way to Seattle."

"That's a lie!" he brayed. "We know what happened to that gold. You sent it downriver with that dirty French-Injun, Roche. He took it in his *bateau,* didn't he? And now you're plannin' on hittin' it down the long coulée to meet him." For the first time he noticed the outfit Nivens was wearing. "Sure . . . see what he's got on. Dressed for the trail!"

A mutter ran through the crowd. Some of those still on the sidewalk tried to crowd inside, pushing the others farther into the room.

Nivens glanced around for Carpenter, the U.S. marshal. Nowhere in sight. He laughed. The fellow had ducked out the back door.

"You see somethin' funny about this?" McSloy barked.

"I see something funny about you. You and your mob. You haven't got guts to hang a man. You haven't got guts to come up here after me, not any one of you, or all of you together. Now take your yellow-gutted mob and get it off my property."

McSloy should have charged forward or gone for his gun. Instead, he hesitated. The hesitation was only momentary, but it could be noticed. The broad, red-faced operator named

Crawford flung Haugen from his way and shouted: "We wasted enough time talkin'! If you boys ain't got the guts to go up there . . . !"

"Crawford, I wouldn't want to kill you." Nivens sounded quiet and sincere.

"I got a gun." Crawford jerked open his Mackinaw revealing a Colt revolver thrust in the band of his pants.

"It's a cold country to lie dead in," Nivens said.

Crawford made no move to draw. He wouldn't, either. Nivens could tell that by his eyes.

VII

The mob was ready to back out. It's one thing to go on an emotional spree and stretch rope with some poor devil's neck, but it's something else when you start risking your own hide. They felt empty where the fire of anger had been, and some of them already began edging to the door. But men outside were still pushing, their voices raised with new excitement. A man was crowding through the door. The newcomer was Colin Starr.

"Nivens!"

"I'm right here."

McSloy turned and peered at Starr. His loose face looked more than ever surly and beaten. Starr's arrival was just the final evidence of his failure. McSloy muttered a vile word under his breath, but nobody was paying any attention to him now.

Starr walked to the foot of the stairs, stood with his left hand on the banister, his right hanging at his side. He'd removed his mittens and stuffed them in his Mackinaw pocket. The Mackinaw was unbuttoned.

The two men met each others gaze. "Better think it over, Nivens," Starr said.

"I have."

The tone, rather than the words themselves, carried Nivens's meaning.

"Don't be a fool," Starr said.

Nivens kept looking at Starr, but his voice was sharp, and his words meant for the crowd. "You're here for your boss, aren't you? For Lester Bohne. Why didn't he come himself? Didn't he have the guts?" He lifted his eyes and looked around the crowd. "Know who this is, boys? This fellow who calls himself Barnes? He's just modest. His real name is Colin Starr. Colin Starr of Cheyenne. The one and only. I thought you'd like to know. Colin Starr who's rented his gun one time or another to the highest bidder in every mine war in the West. Now he's here to kill me." He laughed again. He even managed to sound amused.

"Don't be a fool," Starr repeated under his breath. "I don't want to kill you, Nivens."

The crowd had become restive at talk of killing, and by now both men were given plenty of room with no one even remotely in the line of fire.

"Then get out," Nivens said.

"Be smart." Starr placed one foot on the stair, but he stopped without mounting. His voice was inaudible to anyone but Nivens. "Bohne will make a cash settlement. Go over and see him."

"I said to get out."

"You've been asking for it, Nivens. I knew how it would be that first day."

Nivens turned as though to climb the stairs. His movement was apparently casual, but something about it sprang the hair-triggered tension of Colin Starr's nerves. He twisted, hand coming up inside his Mackinaw. But still he'd been fooled. He'd been watching Nivens's right hand, and in turning Nivens's left had been momentarily hidden. It was the left hand that went to the shoulder holster. The silver-mounted .32 had cleared its leather before Starr had barely started his draw. Nivens's gun pounded, sending a streak of powder flame beneath his uplifted right arm.

Starr had turned slightly with his draw. The .45 Colt was out, but not leveled. Nivens's .32 slug tore down between hammer and stock of the heavier gun, striking between Star's thumb and forefinger, glancing from his wrist. The gun fell. He was still on his feet. Crouched, right wrist clutched in his left hand, his face momentarily twisted in resignation to pain. Then he let the wounded arm dangle at full length, blood running in a rapid stream from the tips of his fingers.

"Handkerchief," he whispered to himself. He repeated: "Handkerchief . . . handkerchief. . . ." He fumbled through pants pockets. The .32 hung in Nivens's hand, pointed at the stairs. Starr still fumbled. He had forced a grin to his teeth.

"That's the trouble with you, Nivens. You're good with a gun, but somebody's going to kill you. It isn't a fast draw that makes a gunman. It's a willingness to shoot to kill. That's the difference between you and me." He still used his good hand, fumbling from one pocket to the other. His face had quit showing pain, but it still had the peculiar, gray tenseness caused by bullet shock. "I never shoot at bottles."

His hand was clutched in his Mackinaw pocket. Explosion of a heavy Derringer tore his pocket, but Nivens had already flung himself aside. Nivens's foot slipped and he half fell. His elbow was propped against a stair when he fired the .32 again.

Starr reeled from the force of the bullet. His eyes looked like milky quartz, but he was still fumbling in his pocket. The .32 exploded again. It drove Starr to the wall.

Starr clawed, fingernails leaving streaks on the wall's unpainted planks. He sat down, one leg folded under him. His expression would have brought a guffaw had it been presented on the stage of the Slipper, but there, with bullets smashed through him, it had a stunning, hypnotic effect on the crowd.

His left hand popped into sight leaving the Derringer behind. Smoke of black powder and scorched wool floated up from his pocket.

"I always knew you carried that ace in the hole, Colin," Nivens said. But Colin Starr was beyond hearing.

Nivens reloaded the three empty chambers, doing it by feel, his eyes not leaving the crowd beneath him. If anything more were needed to take the guts out of them, sight of the killing had done it. Nivens *clicked* the swing-out cylinder back with his thumb, re-holstered the gun in its shoulder grab. "All right, boys. The show's over. Get out. And take your gunman with you."

Not once since the last shot was fired did Nivens look at Starr. He backed up the stairs, eyes straight ahead. His face looked lean and older, his lips were a bloodless straight line beneath his trimmed moustache.

Men had charged up the rear stairs at sound of shooting, and now they were in the upper hall, watching him.

"Get out!" he said.

They'd been posted by the rear door to prevent his escape, but they could see that everything had changed.

Now that he was out of sight, everyone in the front room had something to say. He could even hear the braying tones of McSloy, boasting despite the defeat he had suffered.

Nivens hurried out the rear door. The wind was carrying snow in dense billows. It had seemed hot inside, a nauseating closeness, and the sharp north wind helped. He buttoned his Mackinaw and crossed to Front Street.

He walked from one dive to the next, looking for Senator Otman. Men kept passing him, hurrying toward the First National. Some of the places were empty even of bartenders. No sign of the senator. It occurred to him that Putois Charley might be back. But he was not at the California.

Loftus saw him and walked over. "You'd better blow this camp. It's too hot for you."

Nivens laughed. "I thought I was too hot for it."

"Don't be a fool. Bohne will smoke you out if he has to do it himself."

"Putois Charley hasn't been back?"

"No."

"Get the senator out of the way if you see him."

"The senator will be all right. All the boys like him."

"Anyhow, keep him staked this winter." He drew a Seattle cashier's slip from his billfold. "The senator can endorse this and make it negotiable, but give it to him as he needs it. Otherwise he'll have every dance-hall girl on Front Street high on champagne for one happy night."

He left by the rear door. It seemed that the snow was increasing from minute to minute, swinging on wind eddied from nearby roofs, flying off into darkness. He paused by the glow of a window and looked at his watch. Half an hour had passed since that fracas at the First National. He'd wasted too much time already. The sleds would be at Porthill, waiting.

Wind made a roaring sound through frozen cottonwood branches along the riverbank, but the snow seemed to lessen as soon as he was beyond range of the lights on Front Street. Putois Charley should have returned by then and his canoe should have been moored at the docks a couple of hundred yards below the river house. It wasn't. He saw only a couple of whipsawed plank skiffs frozen in young ice that was forming despite the wind.

He started back. Men were still running along the platform sidewalks. Things would be popping in Scratchgravel. Bohne and the commissioner could give things a flavor of genuine legality now they had a dead man to show.

Someone had walked in view along the side street, paused,

and went on toward the river house. He recognized Joan Crandall and hurried to intercept her.

"Oh, thank God! I'd given up hopes of finding you." She stopped with hands resting on the breast of his Mackinaw. He noticed she was shivering—but from excitement rather than cold.

"What is it?" he asked.

"They have the senator over there."

"Who? Carpenter?"

"No. McSloy. They brought him here. They made him tell what you were doing with the gold. That's why I had to find you."

"So the senator talked."

"Don't blame him. It was awful. I came in the side door and saw it. They struck him. . . ."

"McSloy?"

"No. It was Lester. Lester Bohne. He did it." She was looking at him with intense, still-horrified eyes. "It was awful. He struck him. That poor old man. Struck him down and kicked him."

"How long ago was it?"

"I don't know. I went from there to the First National. It was full of men. Then I walked all the way across town to the California. I knew he was your friend . . . that man who owns the California. He wouldn't tell me where you were."

Her small hands were still clutching the front of his Mackinaw. It gave him the sense of how alone she was in that raw, rough camp.

"You think the senator's in any danger?"

She shook her head. "He was bleeding . . . around the mouth. He staggered outside. That man . . . McVey . . . was with him."

"McVey will take care of him."

She paused a moment, stood with wind blowing the wolverine

118

fur of her parka hood. She asked: "What are you going to do now?"

"I'm going outside, over the Richardson Trail and down to tidewater. There'll be a steamer there in a week or ten days. It'll wait for the gold at Valdez. We can go back to the States on her."

She was staring at him. He didn't know whether the suggestion had surprised her or not.

"You can't just stay here," he told her. "You know what Bohne is like."

"Yes, I know."

"You'll have to get a few things. I'll take you up to your home."

"I don't want to go back there!"

It was the first he'd taken special notice—she was dressed in winter garb, moccasins, heavy wool stockings, a long parka. The dog drivers would have extra clothing if she needed it.

She said: "I have a brother in Skagway. If you could. . . ."

"We'll talk about that later. We have to blow this camp. We need a canoe. My freight sleds are upriver at Porthill Landing. If we can't find a canoe, then we'll have to make it overland."

Men were still hurrying along Front Street, headed toward the Bohne mercantile. A posse would be forming. It was no longer a secret where the gold was being held. Bohne had convinced lots of them Nivens was a thief, and they would be determined to get it back.

"We'll have to hurry," he said, taking her arm, pulling her around.

They went down the slight slope to the river house. A foot-deep drift had settled on the lee side. Generally a couple of company canoes would be tied to the pilings, but they were gone, probably inside the boathouse.

He tried the big, suspended warehouse doors. Barred on the

inside. He cursed. It would be an all-night trip through timber, rock, and snow to Porthill, and Bohne, with his canoes, would reach it ahead of him.

A light was burning behind frost-covered windows in the wharf shanty. Nivens didn't want to start a commotion. But there was no other way. He reached inside his parka, drew his revolver.

Joan grabbed his wrist. "I'll get the canoe."

Nivens let her go. He stood in the shadow of a hand winch as she walked to the door, opened it. For a few seconds she was silhouetted in yellow candlelight talking to old Bill Adams, the wharf tender. She went inside, and after a while he could hear them inside the long warehouse.

It seemed to take a long time. He waited with no sound but the storm rising and falling, the steady roar of current and waves. He kept thinking of Bohne and his posse at the company store, wondering when he'd get them started. He'd hand-pick the gang and come to the river house.

One of the doors *creaked* open and Adams staggered into sight carrying one of the long canoes over his head.

"Excusin' me, ma'am," he said, grunting, propping one end of the craft against the river house wall to keep it from whipping away in the wind. "Excusin' me, but this is one hell of a night for anybody to go out in a canoe. You're sure the boss wanted me to stick 'er in the water? Look at that young ice, ma'am. She's there, a couple inches under the surface with the waves kickin' over her. Sharp as a Cree knife, that ice is, and it'll cut the side out of this canoe with one whack. Nobody'd stand a show if he got dumped in that kind of water. Worse'n breakin' through in midwinter. And at night. . . ."

"I said to put it in the water. He was in a hurry!"

Adams grunted something, but he gave in. "All right, Miss Crandall. I just work here. If the boss said so, I guess maybe he knows what he's doin'. There, she won't freeze up for an hour or so, less'n the wind dies."

She took the babiche mooring line from his hands. "Go uphill and tell him it's ready. He's at the commissioner's house. If he isn't there, wait for him."

Adams peered at her from under gray eyebrows. He'd turned and was almost facing Nivens who stood in the shadow of the hand winch barely two steps away. Adams muttered something and walked past without noticing.

Nivens grabbed the babiche line. The canoe had swung close in and was rubbing its side against ice that clung in ragged points to the pilings.

"You first."

She slid over the edge, stood for a moment in the jiggling craft, then sat cross-legged, taking one of the paddles. In doing it, she showed some experience on water, and he was thankful. He swung down beside her, coiling the babiche. The canoe swung lazily, feeling for the current.

"Mid-river," he said. "Adams was right about that young ice. It could carve this canoe like an axe."

They seemed to be poised, motionless, with the river house slipping away in the dark. Lights from Front Street made streaks of white as they caught the reflections of a billion snowflakes. Wind kept swinging the craft, driving it toward the south bank and it was a continual fight with paddles to keep it in mid-river.

Bluff shadow cut off view of the town, but even on that darkest night there was still a glow rising from snowy bluffs and the river.

It was an hour to Porthill Landing, although the canoe almost overshot it in the storm.

"Here it is!" Nivens said. He brought the canoe around sharply, and groped for the log float. Ice had frozen along it, and the craft struck with a ripping sound. Someone was running up in the dark.

"*Halte-la!*" It was a nasal, French voice, emphasized by the *clatter* of a rifle lever. "It's me."

"*Eh?*"

The man came forward, looking huge and hump-shouldered in his flapping canvas parka. "*Eh . . . bein.* We theenk perhaps you come tomorrow." He looked at the girl but resisted asking a question.

"Did Putois Charley get here?"

"Sure. He mebby-so asleep. I don' know."

"Sleds ready?"

"*Eh?* You need heem more snow for sled."

"We'll have to get going, snow or not. Bohne will be out here trying to stop me in another hour."

The camp was hidden by jack timber a half mile up Porthill Creek. Staked out malemutes set up a wild barking when they came up.

"Who thees?" A man crawled from the folds of a rabbit-skin blanket. It was Pierre Roche, the boss dog driver and one of the French-Canucks who had squared logs for the strongbox. "*Eh . . .* so. You come. Nivens, François, *ma'mselle.*" It was as though he had expected the girl all along. He was grinning, showing his strong teeth. "Maybe they notice of black sand in vault, hey? Maybe we hit trail queek?"

VIII

The sleds were ready, standing beneath canvas covers in the dark. There was a wild mix-up as drivers fought and kicked the wolf-wild malemutes getting them into the tugs.

Pierre was bellowing: "You, François, get thees lead team out. Mush! Mush!"

François rocked the sled free of its set and heaved on the

handles while malemutes hit the breast bands. The sled got going with its small but heavy cargo, its runners grating on stones, then it ran with cushioned ease in deeper snow around a contour of the hillside.

The second team went out five minutes later, the third, and the fourth—that last loaded with dried fish, and caribou, and rabbit-skin blankets—supplies for the long trip.

"There it goes," said Nivens. "Half a million in gold." He looked down on the girl's face. "You don't think I'm going down the owlhoot coulée with it, do you?"

"What do you mean?"

"You don't think I'm stealing it."

"Of course not!"

The snow in most places was now six or seven inches deep and light as goose down. Sometimes a sled runner would *ring* sharply on an exposed rock, but for the most part it was easy going around side hills with the creek close below. After an hour the creekbed narrowed, and they pointed toward the high country.

It became a brutal, incessant struggle through timber, across feeder gullies. The night seemed endless. It had been three years since Nivens had traveled hard, and he could feel this in the backs of his legs, in the straining muscles of his back.

He stopped in the partial wind shelter of a spruce tree, lighted a match, kept its wind-blown flame alight long enough to glimpse the hands of his watch. It was 4:08.

"Tired?" he asked, looking down at the girl.

"No!"

She said it too forcefully.

"It's best to take it a little easy the first day. We've leveled off now and the snow isn't bad. You'd better grab a lift in the hamper of that cargo sled."

"I'm not tired!"

Spirit, or maybe she was telling the truth. Women sometimes fool men with their endurance.

"All right. We'll camp at daylight, or whenever we get to Tesleet."

"Is that Halfway House?"

"I wish it was. Tesleet is nothing but a shanty, even if it is marked on the maps. Government survey shack. Or maybe it's been blown away."

It had been hell, that six or seven miles up from the gulch of Porthill, but here it was rolling country on the divide between Porthill and the Scratchgravel, with the hills of the Delta River lying beyond. It was still snowing but the wind was dying when gray dawn filtered through.

"We on the trail?" Nivens asked Pierre Roche.

"Ees no trail. Just way to get there." He grinned from the circle of a parka hood that was thrust back as though it were too hot for his big, red face. "We get to Valdez, all right. You jus' follow Pierre!"

Wind kept blowing holes in the storm, giving fragmentary glimpses of the benches over which they had climbed. No sign of pursuit. They sighted a cabin almost buried in drifts of new snow among leafless cottonwoods in a gulch bottom. It was Tesleet, the shanty put up two years before by the Army survey crew.

The dogs were fed frozen strips of caribou. Inside, a Frenchman named Mercier prepared tea, bacon, bannock bread. They slept—then the trail again through waning afternoon. It was better traveling through night twilight than by day with the glare on the snow. Deep midnight—they paused again, brewed tea, ate thawed beans and bannock in the shelter of spruce trees by a tiny frozen lake.

While others rested, Nivens climbed a promontory and looked across starlit miles of the back trail, watching for the string of dark dots that would be a pursuing dog team. Nothing.

The trail again. Deep snow was forcing Joan to spend more time riding the sled hamper, for the big Cree snowshoes were too large for her to manage. Sun rose for its brief autumn appearance, turned the world to glaring white. On the southern horizon, picked up and made grayish by the sun, rose a trail of wood smoke.

"Halfway House?" Nivens asked, coming up on his long webs to stand beside Pierre Roche.

"No. Thees look like camp smoke. Perhaps one those Chechako prospector." He spat. "Chechako prospector all over country now."

Halfway House was farther to the west. The trail took them around wooded hillsides.

Arctic day vanished, leaving in its place a long twilight bright enough for a man to read by. Stars were out. They descended to some broad beaver meadows.

One of the stars seemed large and yellowish, deep-set along the horizon. It took Nivens a while to realize it was not really a star, but a lighted window.

"Halfway House," said one of the French-Canucks.

The light kept disappearing and coming again as the trail wound through miles of timber. Then, unexpectedly, it was close with the cabin's snow-covered roof outlined against dark spruce trees.

Nivens was at the lead sled. He instructed Pierre Roche to wait and started on alone.

"Don' worry about squawman at Halfway," Pierre said. "Ol' Jeff Goff all right. I know heem long tam."

"I'll have a look around anyhow."

He walked through jack spruce timber with snowshoes settling four or five inches deep. Timber hid him from the dog teams, and from the cabin ahead. It was farther than he expected. Perhaps half a mile. He climbed a steep pitch from the creekbed and paused at the edge of a clearing.

Halfway House was a long, low cabin with a pole awning built along one side to keep the deep snow of those altitudes from packing in and blocking the entrances. Windows of oiled caribou skin glowed with firelight. It seemed more dim and brownish than it had at a distance. Sparks were drifting from the big stone chimney.

Behind the cabin were the usual outbuildings—dog pens and sheds, a summer ice well, the cache house on stilts with moose antlers reared high like the figurehead of a ship. He stood in timber for about ten minutes. There was no movement, no sound except for the occasional whimper of a malemute bedded for the night.

He half circled the clearing. No sled track. Only a snowshoe trail leading down to beaver meadows. It looked safe enough.

He walked across the clearing with starlight revealing him sharply against the snow. Hard to keep from thinking of an ambush bullet, especially as he approached the midway point in the clearing where an ambusher would be most likely to put him down. Nothing—no movement. Just a malemute in the pens that caught scent of him and set up a commotion.

A path, deep-trodden in snow, led down beneath the pole awning and to the door. He bent to untie the lashings of his snowshoes, then he rapped.

"Come in!" a voice said.

It was unfamiliar and gruff. He pulled a babiche string and the wooden latch came up, letting the door *creak* open. Mist formed in a quick billow when cold struck the slightly steamy air of inside, then it vanished, and his eyes swept the long room.

He could see two persons—a big, whiskered, rough-looking

man just rising from his chair by a table, and a greasy Siwash squaw.

The man let his tangle of red whiskers revolve around a chew of tobacco, spat on the floor, and said: "Well, come on in! I ain't choppin' wood to heat the whole Chisana."

Nivens walked on inside, shoved the door shut with his heel, pushed back the hood of his parka so its fur edgings would not interfere with his vision. The whiskered man was giving him an intent scrutiny, his jaw rapidly working on the tobacco.

"Where's your outfit?"

Nivens met his eyes. It seemed like a peculiar question, coming the way it did. "Maybe I haven't got any."

The man grunted. "I ain't tryin' to horn in on your business. It's just that I didn't hear no dog string. Maybe you left it somewhere and come on by yourself. I got a 'breed boy out in the shack. He ain't done a bit o' work all day. He'll go and fetch it along."

"Why would I leave my outfit and come here alone? What's on your mind?"

"Damn it all!" The man shrugged, turned, and spat at the fire. Its flames gave his face a ruddy cast, like tarnished bronze. He was a heavy man, about forty, with blunt features that would generally indicate an easy-going nature. But he wasn't easy-going tonight.

The squaw was standing by the fire. She hadn't moved once. Her face was expressionless.

The man grunted. "Name's Goff."

"Nivens."

They shook hands. There was something about his eyes. A narrowness, a speechless entreaty—a warning. There was something he wanted to say and couldn't.

Goff cleared his throat: "Say your outfit was outside?"

"It'll be along . . . when I go after it." Nivens smiled, and went on: "I dare say if somebody shoots me in the back, it won't be along at all."

Goff tried to laugh. He said something, but Nivens, peeling his parka off, couldn't hear what it was. He unbuttoned his Mackinaw, glanced at Goff again. The man was staring straight at him, but the squaw's eyes were on something beyond his back. He knew, then, even before the cabin's silence was broken by the metallic *click* of a gun hammer.

"Lester?" he asked.

"Yes." Lester Bohne's voice.

Nivens turned and faced him.

Bohne had stepped from behind a bear robe that draped the door to a storeroom. He was holding a Colt revolver waist high. His face looked leaner and more savage than before.

"How did you know I was here?" Bohne asked, trying to make his tone as easy as Nivens's.

Nivens laughed. "I used to live in a rattlesnake country. They have an odor about them. A man never forgets."

Bohne's lips peeled back in what was intended to be a smile, but he seemed to be losing the fight to control his fury. "Trying to talk yourself into an ounce of bullet lead?"

"No. I didn't figure you'd shoot me. You must want me alive for a while or you'd have pulled that bushwhack trigger when I walked in the door."

"All right. I do want you alive." He jerked the Colt muzzle, indicating Nivens's shoulder holster. "You have a gun there. Take it out. With two fingers."

"Sure."

Nivens reached beneath his Mackinaw, lifted the .32 as Bohne had instructed, dropped it muzzle first to the floor. Then he kicked it aside for good measure. It struck the wall. Bohne just left it there. He glanced at the squawman and his wife.

"Sit down."

They obeyed, seating themselves on a bench by the fire.

Bohne said: "That was a foolish business back in Scratchgravel. You killing Colin Starr. Killing is always foolish. And unnecessary. It never settles anything."

Nivens smiled and made his old, habitual movement of smoothing one forefinger over his moustache. "Colin thought it did . . . or else why would he have come around to kill me? And you have a gun in your hand."

"It never settles anything. It never brings a man what he wants. Look at us here. Killing you would never get me the thing I want most. I might as well admit it, because you know it anyway."

Nivens knew what he meant. It would only make Joan Crandall hate him, if she didn't hate him already.

Bohne said: "I told Starr I was willing to make a deal with you. I told him to tell you that. Did he?"

"He told me, and I said you could take your deal and go to hell. He went for his gun."

"Guns were his business."

"There's no use of talking about it now. I probably liked Colin better than you did. You had something to say to me. What was it?"

"Why, that deal I wanted to make with you in Scratchgravel. I'm still willing. I'll buy the First National for more than it's worth. I'll give you an order on my Seattle account for two thousand ounces of gold. That represents a lot of money. Better than thirty-three thousand dollars."

"And this shipment I'm taking through? How about that?"

"Why, that isn't yours. It belongs to the First National. I'll become responsible for it. If I want to send it on through by dog teams, I'll do it. Or if I think it's safer to keep it in Scratchgravel till the river opens, I'll do that, too."

"And of course there's one other thing. . . ."

"Miss Crandall will return to her father."

"You'd better ask her."

"Damn it, Nivens, I'm trying to get along with you."

"And I'm trying to be considerate of the girl. She doesn't want to go back to her father."

Bohne's lips were drawn thin, twisted down. He hissed: "But it would be all right for her to stay with you."

"She has a brother in Skagway. Once she's outside, she can go there, or to Seattle. Whatever she wants."

"You expect me to believe that? Don't you think I know what you want? Don't you think I know what a tinhorn sport like you intends with that young girl?"

"You have a dirty mind, don't you?"

"I also have a gun."

"I'm well aware of that."

"There's no use of bickering. I have the drop on you. It's one of the hard facts of this situation. In the eyes of the law, you are a murderer. It's open season on you. On you and the gray wolves. I've made a fair offer. If you refuse it, there's only one thing left for me to do."

"Sure you can kill me. Remember, though, neither Joan nor my outfit is here."

"I can back trail and find it."

"Do you think I'd be fool enough to start over the Richardson with two tons of gold and no gun guard. I have the men to put up a fight. You'd never get close enough to spring an ambush, malemutes' noses being what they are. Somebody would get killed. Maybe it would be my boys, or yours, or both. Anyhow, you said something about killing never settling anything."

"Your answer is no?"

"It's no."

Bohne's eyes roved the room, came to rest on the squared log mantle.

"Bring the cards," he growled.

Goff carried them over, put them down, backed away.

Bohne sat looking at the deck. It was old and greasy, twice the thickness of a new deck. He picked it up, shuffled, placed it in the middle of the table.

"You have a reputation for wagering against these things."

Nivens nodded. He scarcely glanced at the cards. He was leaning back in the rough, homemade chair, watching Bohne's eyes.

Bohne said: "All right. If you're a gambling man, I'll play you one hand. For everything. I'll go you one better. I'll cut the cards. High card. Winner goes home . . . alone. Or haven't you that kind of intestines?"

Nivens barely smiled. "There should be a mortgage, too. I seem to remember this scene from the old Alessandro Theater in San Francisco. Walter Nesbitt in the *Wolf of Wall Street.*"

"You never saw this scene in the Alessandro."

Nivens looked down at the cards. He reached for them to shuffle.

"No!"

He took his hands back.

"I know your reputation with cards. We'll cut them the way they are." Bohne jerked his head: "Go on. Cut!"

Nivens reached with a careless movement, broke the deck near its bottom, faced a card. It was the king of hearts.

Bohne stared down on the grimy pasteboard. His face looked more lean and hollow, firelight striking across it, accentuating his hard-set jaw and prominent forehead. Anyone casually glancing at him would think he still had control over his emotions, but Nivens had long practice in reading truth from little things, and he saw the rapid throb of the little artery along his temple, the rigidity of neck muscles, the set tenseness of fingers as he reached for the deck.

He cut the cards, hesitated a second, flipped them over. Lying face up atop the greasy half deck was the four of spades.

IX

Bohne stood up. He was hunched, staring hard at the card. His hand swung down, seized the card atop the remainder of the deck. He looked at it, crumpled it, hurled it away. That card was the ace of hearts. He'd planted that ace, but he'd made the error of cutting the card above.

Nivens pretended not to notice. He stood up.

"Well?"

"Don't grin at me!" Bohne fairly screamed. "You dirty, rotten tinhorn. You knew where that king was . . . !"

"How could I? You didn't even let me put my hands on the deck."

Bohne backed away, the six-shooter still clutched in his big hand. He stood, spread-legged, in the middle of the room. He got hold of himself. "All right. You win, Nivens. I won't bother you any more."

There was something in the way he said it, coming down strongly on the I.

"Can I have my gun?"

"Go ahead."

He watched closely, six-gun ready. Nivens retrieved his .32, put it back in the holster. He didn't button the Mackinaw. His parka was lying over a chair. He picked it up, started for the door.

With a solid stride Bohne got there ahead of him, flung the door open. He lifted his hand with a flourish. He was smiling, dramatic and cynical. He bowed.

"This is good bye for good, Nivens. I'm getting rid of you the hard way, but it's better than not getting rid of you at all."

The gesture was out of Bohne's character. The hand flung

high—more like a signal. In going through the door, Nivens would momentarily be in full silhouette against the fire. He seemed about to make the step, but at the final instant he twisted aside, flattened himself to the casing. The air fluttered inches away, and the rocking *ka-whang* of a high-powered rifle reached him an instant later.

Nivens had paused only momentarily. He pivoted, rolled off the wall. He glimpsed Bohne turning, trying to bring the .45 Colt to aim. Nivens struck the floor. Concussion filled the room. Close range. He could feel the sting of burning powder, the rip of splinters torn from the floor beneath his hands.

He rolled with second and third slugs *thudding* the log wall, came to a crouch in the momentary concealment of the shoulder-high box that Goff used for his grub storage. The room was filled with a choking smell of gunsmoke. The door was still open. He could feel cold draft around his feet.

The big grub box hid him, but it was no real protection against a bullet. Just sheet metal nailed over a pole frame designed to frustrate the claws of mice and pack rats. Beyond the grub box was a wooden bench, and farther the door to the storeroom where Bohne had been concealed.

There had been some bales of fur stored near the door. Those packed furs would make excellent protection, and he had little doubt Bohne had chosen to place himself there.

Nivens held the .32 in his right hand. He started to rise, to move aside. The plank floor trembled, and there was a little, tinny sound from the grub box. Concussion ripped the room again. The bullet tore through metal, drilling the box dead center.

Slivers of metal tore at Nivens's cheek. He twisted into the open as Bohne fired again. He was certain the man would be crouched behind the baled furs. He realized as he fired that no one was there. Bohne was in the partial protection of an upended chair. And directly behind him, at one side of the fire, staring though apparently as phlegmatic as ever, was the Siwash squaw.

No chancing a shot. He sprang forward, low to the floor. The maneuver was totally unexpected. Bohne hesitated an instant, trying to tilt the muzzle of his gun. Time was too short. Flame from the gun brushed across Nivens's shoulders, and he struck Bohne at almost the same instant.

Momentum carried the big man to the wall. In the first second of struggle, Bohne pulled the Colt's trigger again. The hammer *clicked*—empty. He flung the gun away, seized Nivens's wrist, fought for the .32.

They reeled across the room. Bohne's weight was making itself felt. He was stronger than Nivens. He spread his powerful legs, bent Nivens's right arm slowly, forced it toward his spine, sought a hammerlock. Nivens let the gun fall. He tried to twist around, but the maneuver came too late. His bent right arm made him a prisoner.

Bohne wheezed from effort, clutched Nivens close with one arm, reaching around to apply pressure to the hammerlock with the other. Pain from the tortured shoulder socket sent waves of blindness across Nivens's eyeballs.

He swung his left fist, aiming for Bohne's guts. Bohne took the blow against the stiffened wall of his abdomen. His face was thrust close, lips peeled from his teeth, grinning.

"Your punch hasn't much steam tonight!" he hissed.

Bohne rammed the arm higher. He was trying to break it, to twist it free of its socket. But he was in the wrong position. Nivens was too tall; the reach was too far. He was reaching with his left arm, putting the pressure on Nivens's right. He changed hands. For a moment the hammerlock relaxed. Nivens tried to get his arm down, but it seemed to be paralyzed. Bohne's laugh was guttural in his ear. At last Bohne had it the way he wanted.

From the past, a picture flashed through Nivens's brain, a memory of Gotch being held in the same hold at the arena in Leadville. As Bohne thrust up with final, bone-snapping power, Nivens sprang aside, and just like Gotch's toe had hooked a rope of the wrestling ring, Nivens's moccasin found momentary purchase on the table's edge.

Bohne still held his wrist, but Nivens's maneuver had taken the pressure off his shoulder. He twisted his entire body around, bringing the hammerlocked arm to his side. Then he lunged forward, shoulder smashing to the pit of Bohne's stomach.

Bohne let go, staggered to the wall. He struck it, rebounded. He was fighting to get breath in his lungs. He saw Nivens in front of him and tried to raise his arms.

Nivens brought his left fist up, and the blow smashed Bohne's head to one side. He punched with the right, the left again.

Strength was flowing back through his right arm and shoulder. Bohne had taken the three blows and was still up. He wasn't licked—just off balance. He aimed a wild haymaker.

Nivens moved just enough to make it miss. The force of it carried Bohne halfway around. Nivens hesitated, set his feet, and swung with perfect timing, dropping the big man with a right to the face. Bohne's falling weight raised dust from the floor cracks. He got to his feet, eyes glazed, one arm groping. Nivens smashed him again. He fell, the force of the blow sending him on his back. His head struck the far wall and he was limp, eyes still open, blood running from one corner of his mouth.

Nivens steadied himself, holding the edge of the table. Punishment and fatigue had made him dizzy.

Goff, the squawman, shouted something. The outside door was still open. A man was out there—a man crossing beneath the pole awning—snow-covered planks *creaking* beneath his moccasins.

Nivens spun around, expecting another bullet. He glimpsed the gun on the floor. His own gun, the .32. He dove, came up from the table's momentary concealment with it in his hand. The man was through the door, rifle held hip high, peering at the limp form of Lester Bohne. It was McSloy. He looked around the room, and for the first time noticed Nivens—and the .32.

McSloy stopped. His loose face was twisted with brutish fear. He dropped the rifle.

"I should shoot your lights out," Nivens said.

McSloy opened his mouth, but no sound came. Terror had turned his face into something inhuman. He rolled his head back and forth in a negative movement, eyes fixed on the gun muzzle. His mouth gaped open and closed again three times before he could force a sound from his throat.

"No. No. Don't shoot. I didn't do nothin'. I never meant you no harm. Honest. Listen, Nivens. . . ."

"You were outside waiting for Bohne's signal. You tried to put a slug through me."

"No I didn't. I missed, didn't I? I could have shot you if I'd wanted. Sure I could have. I could have blasted hell out of you. I didn't want to hit you. You gotta believe me, Nivens. Bohne planted me out there, said he'd give me the high sign if you didn't settle peaceful. But. . . ."

Nivens laughed.

"No. Nivens, listen. I'll tell you all about that dirty. . . . ." He jerked his head at Bohne and called him a vile name. "Listen. I'll tell you plenty about him. You know why he had to get hold of this shipment of gold? This gold you're mushin' to Valdez? He kept it quiet, but his whole summer consignment went down off Port Anvik. Lost every color in the quicksand. Them Siwash out at Likwalla was pickin' up pieces of that riverboat for a week. Didn't dare let news leak out yet on account of the insurance. Payin' it'd break him. Fact is, he couldn't pay it, but the commission on this gold you got might pull him through."

"Are you telling the truth?"

"Honest, Nivens."

Yes, McSloy, was telling the truth. Nivens could tell it by his eyes. He put the gun away.

McSloy was filled with relief. "Sure, and I'll tell you more, too. Listen here, did you know how Joe Lestrup happened to die? Called it pneumonia, but he'd been cracked up in a fight with Bohne. Bohne had got him down and caved his slats in, and. . . ."

He stopped. Bohne had shaken unconsciousness from his brain and was resting on one knee. He'd overheard McSloy's last sentence. His face was twisted with hatred.

"You yellow-belly!" he hissed. "You've messed every job I ever put you on. But you won't sell me out. You won't turn copperhead and write yourself a squealer's ticket out of the country."

McSloy took a step back toward the door. His heel struck the rifle. Bohne was up, ready to charge. McSloy bent, seized the rifle, brought its muzzle up. He pumped the action. There was already a cartridge in the chamber. It flipped high toward the ceiling. Bohne spied his own gun—the Colt revolver. He dove for it, rolled over on the floor, the gun in his hand.

The rifle roared, sending a streak of burning powder across the room's half light. The slug missed narrowly, tearing slivers from the floor a couple of inches from Bohne's elbow.

Bohne turned, leveling the Colt. At the last instant there was an expression like a shadow across his face. Memory that the gun was empty. He worked the mechanism anyway—a final, desperate hope. The hammer *clicked*.

McSloy had reeled to one side as though already struck by the bullet. The empty sound stopped him by the door. He aimed the rifle, paused a moment, and the room was knifed by the second explosion.

It was a soft-nosed bullet. It drove Bohne halfway around. His side collided with the baled furs and they supported him a second or two. He had strength enough to make a tearing motion at his chest, then he sprawled face down, limp, without breath.

McSloy stared at the fallen man. He made sure Bohne was dead. Buck fever suddenly hit him. The rifle almost jumped from his hands. He stared at Nivens

"I kilt him. He's dead, ain't he?"

"He's dead."

"You saw him. He tried to kill me. You was witness, Nivens. You saw yourself. He tried to blast me first. I had to."

There was a technical point involved, thought Nivens. The six-shooter wasn't loaded, but how would McSloy have known that. "Stop worrying, McSloy," Nivens barked.

Nivens could hear leader's bells and the sharp bark of malemutes on the winter air.

Pierre came in sight, long striding with a hand tug over his shoulder.

"*Dieu!* So you live, *m'shu*. We hear shooting."

"Sure, I'm all right."

"What go on in thees Halfway House?"

"It's all happened."

"We stay here now?"

"No. We'll keep straight on up the trail. We'll find a camp spot farther along."

Pierre looked at Nivens but resisted the temptation to ask more questions. "*Eh,* so be it, *m'shu.*"

The other sleds came up, passing Nivens as he stood at one side of the trail. Joan was on the rear runners of the last one.

She saw him and stepped off, sinking deeply in snow.

"You *are* alive! I heard shooting. . . ."

He walked to her, took her mittened hands.

She said: "He was waiting for you?" She was referring to Bohne.

Nivens nodded.

She was close to him, her hands groping the breast of his parka.

"You couldn't help doing it. He'd have killed you. It had to be one of you. It wasn't really killing."

"I didn't kill him."

"Then he's alive?"

"No. He's dead. But I didn't kill him. It was McSloy." McSloy was there, crouched forward, listening. Nivens added for his benefit: "Self-defense."

She exhaled with what sounded like a sob. For a while she stood close, her head pressed tightly against his breast. Some of her hair escaped the parka, and he was conscious of its pine-fresh fragrance.

At last she lifted her face, cheeks glistening from tears. "I'm glad it wasn't you."

Her lips were slightly parted, waiting for him. He knew that McSloy and the grinning French-Canuck dog drivers were watching—knew and didn't care. He felt like one who, after long and futile wandering, had come home.

★ ★ ★ ★ ★

THE CRAFT OF KA-YIP

★ ★ ★ ★ ★

Ka-yip's years were many as the leaves of the chokecherry tree. His skin was browned the color of an old moccasin sole and dehydrated until its wrinkles were infinite and patternless like the skin of a withered potato. Ka-yip sat in the door of his buffalo-skin teepee just behind the woodchopper's shanty and let the morning sunshine sink into his brittle old bones. From time to time he bent forward to inspect a row of cigar butts that were drying on a flat slab of sandstone.

The cigar butts were part of Ka-yip's harvest from the barroom floor of the *Southern Pride,* a Missouri River steamboat that had stopped at the wood lot of his white son-in-law's the day before. They were of many lengths, thicknesses, and colors. There was a thick one that had been less than a third smoked; another, a panatela, had been trod on and shredded by some careless feet; others had been smoked down to their final inch and hence were seasoned a good, rich black. Part of the longest butt was quite dry, so Ka-yip ground it to a leafy pulp between his hard old palms, mixed it with a shred of red willow bark, and loaded the redstone bowl of his pipe.

Ka-yip smoked these long ones first, next those of medium length, and so on down, hoarding the richest and shortest ones throughout the day. Then, as dusk settled over the swift Missouri and its barren bluffs of whitish clay, Ka-yip would savor the good smoke of the shortest and strongest butt of all while he thought deeply of life and its mysteries. Generally, as he sat there in the long twilight, his friend, Wappa-moo, the little gray field mouse, would come for a few last nibbles of food and listen to the wisdom that is the harvest of man's years.

"Behold this cigar butt of the white man," Ka-yip had said the night before, tapping his pipe bowl. "When I picked it up, it was heavy with goodness, and now, dried by the sun, it smokes rich and strong. You would think the white man would treasure such a butt as this, but no. He throws it away!"

At this, Wappa-moo had stopped nibbling for a while and looked up, his little beady eyes shining with comprehension.

"Indeed, Wappa-moo, are not these white men a race of lunatics? These cigars they make at great expense. I have heard it said that the cost of a box of them is as the cost of one cayuse. It would be great wealth to own a dozen of those boxes. And the white men bring them far, carrying them inside a glass case on the boat driven by the great fire. Yet, after all this, they cast away the best part for another to enjoy, like the foolish squaw who took the tail of the buffalo and left the tongue for the magpies."

Before Ka-yip had finished his first morning pipe, there came the jabber of voices and wail of papoose from inside the log house. In a few minutes the stovepipe gave forth smoke, there was an odor of frying food, and soon afterward his daughter, Nis-wah, a name that the white man had shortened to Agnes, came out with a pan of salt pork and doughgods for breakfast.

Ka-yip ate slowly, pulverizing the crisp fat pork between his gums. The doughgods—unleavened flapjacks—were soft and easy to eat. Part of one doughgod he laid aside for the breakfast of his friend, Wappa-moo.

Rupe, Ka-yip's white son-in-law, came from the back door, stretching himself and fingering doughgod from his red whiskers. He was a gangling man of forty or so, long-necked, with a pointed Adam's apple and a complexion that tended to freckle and turn rusty in the sun.

" 'Mornin', Yip." Rupe yawned. "How's the cigar butts holdin' out?"

Rupe always asked that, following up with a snicker that hinted there was something humorous about good, mellowed cigar butts and as though smoking them were beneath his whiteman's pride. Ka-yip deeply resented this tone of his son-in-law's, and he also resented being called Yip. (His name was not Ka-yip even, but Ka-yip-wa-wata-waw-ses-sik which, in the Cree dialect, meant literally "the wise eye", although through usage much more—"the eye of the wise eagle" perhaps, or "the eye and the mind of bravery and wisdom".) It was far too proud a name to be shortened to a mere Yip to please the white man's impatient tongue.

Still, deep as was his resentment, Ka-yip gave no sign. He bowed slightly as was the custom of his tribe and gestured to the cigar butts. "See, *ne koosis,* my son. I have only these."

Rupe yawned again "The *Great West* should be in tomorrow. Maybe you can pick up a few there."

Rupe hitched the bay mare to the Red River cart, tossed in his axe and Henry rifle, and set off toward a grove of big cottonwoods up the coulée. As the Red River cart was made exclusively of two materials, wood and rawhide, the anguish of its axles could be heard long after it had turned a bend and rolled from sight. Wappa-moo, who feared Rupe and the noisy cart, now scurried up through the dry buffalo grass. Ka-yip nodded good morning and commenced rolling up the little ball of doughgod for his little friend's breakfast.

"Behold him, Wappa-moo! Behold my son-in-law, my daughter's husband, that chopper of wood! My family were hunters, and warriors, and mighty stealers of horses, Wappa-moo. Neither my father nor my father's father ever chopped wood for the fire. They would rather lie scalped by Gros Ventres than be seen doing squaw's work. When he came to my lodge, Wappa-moo, and asked for my daughter, I thought him a great hunter . . . a long knife. I thought he was great among his people. But what was he? He was a chopper of wood, an *iskao* weakling."

While Ka-yip sat there, bent forward, savoring his disgrace, his daughter who the white man called Agnes went to the river for a bucket of water. On her way back she paused to look toward the northeast, shading her eyes against the early sun. Ka-yip looked, also. A line of horsemen was approaching across the bench land that sloped down from the low summits of the Bear Paw Mountains.

Ka-yip counted to his last finger. Ten riders. Ten—not since the Blackfoot war party burned the cabin and woodpiles two years before had he seen so many raiders all at once. But these were not Blackfeet. They did not ride long-legged in their saddles, bounding stiff-spined with each jog of the horses—they rode high, taking the jolts with limber knees and sway of hips.

"Behold, Wappa-moo! The white men come, riding like so much boneless meat on their cayuses." Ka-yip made a gesture of misgiving. "It is not well when the white men come in tens without pack horses. It was always such white men without pack horses who took the squaws from our teepees and lifted the hair of our warriors."

Ka-yip puffed his pipe while the riders moved across the bench and descended the trail that crawled like a twisting bull snake down the little badlands hills that separated bench from river. They were white men, as Ka-yip had guessed, a hard, be-whiskered lot, traveling light, save for armament that was unusually heavy and included rifles, pistols, and sawed-off shotguns. In the lead was a long man of hawk-like nose and eye. Seeing Ka-yip, the hawk-like one rode up, lifting his hand, palm first, in a signal of friendship.

"How!" he said.

"How!" answered Ka-yip.

"This is Alkali Coulée landing, ain't it?"

Ka-yip was inscrutable. "No savvy."

The man gestured toward the coulée. "Alkali. Steamboat stop. Heap savvy?"

"No savvy."

A pig-eyed man with a large nose and great, rounded shoulders came forward then to look at Ka-yip and grunt contemptuously: "Hell, Skinner, what's the use of tryin' to talk to an Injun?"

Skinner paid no attention. He tried sign language, gesturing at the dock and forming the figure of a diamond with his two hands. "Diamond B boat stop, savvy?"

Ka-yip watched patiently, but, when Skinner was done, he rocked from side to side and repeated: "No savvy."

The pig-eyed man hee-hawed and beat dust from the leg of his homespun pants. "You sure got aplenty out of him, Skinner." Then in a voice intended for the others to hear: "Any fool would know this was the right place."

Skinner overheard the remark. "Bignose, you're too damned smart. You never been here before. None of us have. If this happens to be the wrong place, that Diamond B boat will wheel right by."

"Don't let me bother you. Go right on, seein' you and gran'pap are gettin' on so well."

Skinner was now more determined than ever to get some information from Ka-yip. He swung down and drew a diagram in the dust, but when he was through, Ka-yip rocked from side to side with sad negation.

"No savvy."

"*Ave-ax el-ax,*" said Skinner, reaching far back in his memory for the words. "*Qhay-ax we-at-ack?*"

"*Kitta meyo kes-i-kaw*," responded Ka-yip.

It was plain that this answer in Cree meant as little to Skinner as his question in Chinook had meant to Ka-yip.

"There's your answer." Bignose snickered, showing a row of decayed teeth.

Suddenly enraged, Skinner drew his heavy cap-and-ball pistol and waggled it under Ka-yip's nose. Ka-yip puffed at his cold pipe and stared unblinkingly at the bluffs beyond the river. "Is this Alkali Coulée?" Skinner asked again.

"No savvy."

Skinner was tempted to pull the trigger, but instead he thrust his foot against Ka-yip's chest with a force that sent him rolling backward, almost into the teepee fire. Ka-yip did not change expression. Slowly, as though his joints were hinges that needed oiling, he resumed his old position and stared out across the river. Skinner thrust the pistol back in its scabbard and looked around at the cabin, the dock, the long woodpiles.

"Where the hell's the wood hawk?" he asked of nobody in particular.

"No savvy," moaned Ka-yip.

"He didn't understand that, neither." Bignose smirked and several of the men laughed.

Skinner spun around. "You don't care much for the way I'm runnin' this, do you, Bignose?"

Bignose was uncomfortable. He showed that in the shiftiness which appeared in his little eyes, but he had a standing to maintain, so he repeated his sarcastic laugh.

"Think you could do it better?" Skinner drew out the words slowly.

A small, gray-whiskered man now spurred his horse between them.

"If you want Old Dad's judgment, you'll hold your temper," he drawled. "We'll need all the men we got before this little piece of business is done. A steamboat is some bigger job than a stagecoach when it comes to liftin' the heavy color."

Bignose and Skinner looked at each other over the neck of Old Dad's horse, but the tension was broken and everyone breathed more easily. They drifted away from the teepee, finally dividing into two groups—Bignose and three others rode up the coulée to find Rupe, while Skinner and the rest loitered around the cabin and the steamboat dock.

They soon brought Rupe back, riding bareback on the old bay horse. His eyeballs had a protruding, frightened look, and he kept gulping as though something had become lodged beneath his Adam's apple.

Now that it was again peaceful near the teepee, Wappa-moo returned for more doughgod.

"Behold these strangers!" said Ka-yip. "They have come here to lie in wait for the boat of the great fire so they can stealum yellow dust that is worth more than horses to the white men. If they do this, Wappa-moo, the boats will be frightened from the wood yard of my son-in-law, for it is said at the lodge fires of my people that the fox which escaped the snare does not travel the same trail again." Ka-yip considered deeply this ancient wisdom. "This is not good, for, if the boats stop coming, there will be no more cigar butts."

Ka-yip wanted to speak of the matter with Rupe, but Rupe did not come near the teepee—he was busy trotting around, doing the bidding of the strangers. Several times Ka-yip signaled, one finger held aloft, but Rupe pretended not to see. It was mid-afternoon before he came close enough for Ka-yip to stop him.

"Those white brothers of yours, *ne koosis*, my son . . . they are bad men. *Meyo-meyo*, heap savvy? It is not good that you stand by while they stealum yellow dust worth more than horses. That is not brave, *ne koosis*, and I know you are a brave man."

"Quiet down," Rupe growled from the side of his mouth, apprehensive of the two men who sat at the back door of the cabin, feasting on dried apples.

"You have wisdom, *ne koosis*. Tell Ka-yip, your father, how you will stop these white men from stealum yellow dust."

"You must think I'm a damned fool. I wouldn't run up against a gang like that for my own money, let alone some heavy color belongin' to a Benton or Saint Louis millionaire."

The bend slowly left Ka-yip's back. "These are not the words of my son! No, this is some stranger I hear speaking!"

"The hell it is!"

"Then you are not a chief?"

"Chief be blowed! I'd ruther be a live woodchopper than Stonewall Jackson in his seven-by-three."

Ka-yip weaved from side to side and moaned.

"You wouldn't be so brave if it was up to you," muttered Rupe defensively.

Ka-yip lifted one forefinger. "*Wache!* I was great brave when the lodges of my people were many like the mounds of the prairie dog town. Once, with only my knife, I rode into a village of Sioux, those eaters of roasted snakes, and stealum five horses. Alone, I did this, *ne koosis,* for I was brave. . . ."

Rupe snorted. "You weren't so brave when the Blackfeet raided a couple summers back. You hightailed it plenty quick that time."

"Rupe!" shouted Bignose. "Get us some more tobacky."

Rupe hopped up obediently, and hurried inside the house for his tin bucket of natural-leaf chewing tobacco. Ka-yip sat watching him while the insult burned into his brain.

"Did you hear what he said, Wappa-moo? He said I ran from the Blackfeet. He said I was not brave. Well, I will show this son-in-law of mine . . . this chopper of wood. I will show him the craft and bravery of the warrior. I will keep watch on these white men. I will trick them so the boats will still come bearing their cigar butts. He will not dare laugh at me tomorrow, Wappa-moo."

Ka-yip sat there, hunched over, seeming to sleep while his shadow grew longer across the ground, and he watched each move, listened to each word of the white strangers.

"Behold these white men, Wappa-moo! Are they not a race of lunatics? They come a long distance to rob the boat of the great fire . . . and of what? I will tell you! To rob it of the yellow metal too soft for knife blade or arrowhead, or anything except the rings on a squaw's finger. These whites! What would they do without their guns that shoot far? They do not have the Cree's bravery or wisdom. No! I would ask nothing easier than to trick them. Once, long ago, a black robe came to our village and told us about these white men. He said that once, far across the great water, there lived the greatest of all white chiefs, a Mana-touwa, who pretended to be poor and went around without eagle feathers in an old capote. Now this white chief did great magic so as to make all the medicine men jealous, and what did they do? They cried out with many lies until the other white men seized the great chief. 'Who are you?' they asked. *'Wache!'* he answered. *'Wache! Keche Ookemawit!* Behold! I am a king!' 'Oh, ha!' laughed these foolish white men, 'see who is here in his old capote and worn-out moccasins saying he is a king! He is a madman, let us nail him to a great tree!' And this they did, these white men. But would he have been treated thus among my people? No, Wappa-moo! We would have honored him, and given him a dry teepee, and feasted him on young boiled dog as we do all madmen. Yet even today these white men look for their great chief to return, but will he come to them? No, he will not. He will come to the Crees who will treat him better." Ka-yip shook his bony old shoulders in a hacking chuckle "Ah, Wappa-moo, I ask nothing easier than to fool such white men."

151

The bandits remained split into two groups—the followers of Bignose and the followers of Skinner, with Old Dad wandering back and forth, attempting to keep the peace. Skinner and his men sat around the woodpiles, on the dock, while the Bignose faction preferred the cabin. Several times Bignose felt of some object inside his shirt, and once, when there was no one around, he drew out a tiny, buckskin bag and peeped inside.

"Did you see him, Wappa-moo?" asked Ka-yip. "Did you see that Bignose peeping into the little sack he keeps tied around his neck? It must be great medicine that he hides it beneath his capote away from even the eyes of his friends. I would give much to know what is in that bag, Wappa-moo."

Ka-yip plotted. He plotted with cunning greater than the lynx cat while the sun swung in its southern arc and slid behind the horizon. Twilight was settling when he signaled with upraised finger to Bignose.

"Wuniska oogemah!" he called.

"What in hell do you want?" Bignose asked.

Ka-yip signaled again, so he walked grudgingly over to the teepee.

Ka-yip looked all around, then he asked in a guarded monotone: "Heap savvy whiskey?"

"Me savvy, but if I had any, I'd drink it myself."

"Me . . . Ka-yip . . . know where plenty whiskey, savvy?"

"Where is it?" asked Bignose with sudden enthusiasm.

Ka-yip assumed a crafty attitude. "Me tell . . . you give . . ."—he gestured with his fingers, one, two, three—*"nestoo mawutche."*

"Three what?"

"You give . . . three dollar."

"You'll get no three dollars from me, you flea-bitten old rag bag. Tell me where it is or I'll wring your neck."

Ka-yip pretended to have great fear. His eyes rolled and he

moaned as he rocked from side to side. "No savvy."

"Where's that likker?"

Ka-yip pointed a trembling finger toward the root cellar. *"Akota watchee."*

"In the root cellar?"

Ka-yip nodded. He spread a ragged fragment of blanket on the ground and peeped under it. *"Akota watchee!"* he repeated.

Bignose hopped up and set off for the root cellar with long strides. He flung open its pole door and leaped into the hole to reappear a moment later with an earthenware jug in each hand.

"Hey, boys!" he bellowed. "Look here what that damned wood hawk had hid on us! Likker . . . gallons of it!"

No bugle ever assembled troops quicker than that cry of "likker" brought the bandits. The jugs commenced passing from hand to hand, and in a short time no hatred, suspicion, or rivalry was left in them. Old Dad was so happy he sang, while others formed sets for an impromptu quadrille. Ka-yip chuckled as he smoked one of the rich, short butts in his redstone pipe.

When darkness settled, the men touched a match to one of Rupe's woodpiles and hilariously kept working on the jugs. Ka-yip covered his teepee fire with dry sod so the coals would hold throughout the night and retired to the heap of buffalo robes that was his bed. He did not lie down. He sat quietly, cross-legged, in the dark, watching the white men through the flap of the teepee.

The woodpile was long, so half the night was over by the time it burned from one end to the other. By that time most of the men were sprawled in various attitudes of alcoholic coma, but three still held on—Bignose, Old Dad, and a man called Dakotah.

Old Dad still sang, lifting his quavering monotone in a popular ditty of the day:

Oh, what was your name in the States?

Dan Cushman

Was it Johnson or Thompson or Bates?
Did you murder your wife
And run for your life?
Say, what was your name in the States?

The sentiment of this song was so overpowering that Old Dad dropped his grizzled head in his hands and wept. Bignose and Dakotah were jangling about the Wingate expedition of 1862 against the Cheyennes. Old Dad wept himself to sleep. Bignose and Dakotah got through the name-calling stage of their dispute without resorting to firearms, and soon they, also, fell asleep.

The coals *crackled* and died down beneath a thick coating of ash. A night breeze sprang up and fluttered the wind sail of the teepee. Ka-yip crept outside and circled the sleeping white men. He found Bignose sprawled out with his feet almost in the warm ashes. Silently as a night hunting weasel Ka-yip crouched and unbuttoned the front of Bignose's shirt, revealing the little buckskin bag nestled in the hair of his chest. Ka-yip was in no hurry to take it. He drew his knife and stropped the blade a few times on his moccasin, then, with two deft movements, he cut the thongs.

He faded back to the shadow of a nearby woodpile, opened the bag, and peeped inside. It contained about twenty bright, many-sided stones of the kind he had seen set in the rings of men and women on the steamboats. Some of them were colorless like ice, while others gleamed red as crystallized blood in the starlight.

Ka-yip took the largest of the stones, a bluish-white one about two-thirds the size of his little fingernail, and hid it under the slab of rock at the door of his teepee. The rest he carried over to where Skinner was snoring near the back door of the cabin and rolled them loosely in the top fold of his buckskin legging. This done, Ka-yip crept back inside his teepee, curled up on his pal-

154

let of buffalo skins, and seemed to sleep.

The last coals of the woodpile died out. The night breeze, sucking down the deep cut of the river, chilled some of the sleepers until they got up and found blankets. Bignose, Skinner, and most of the others slept on while the dawn came up over the Bear Paw Mountains and drove the mist from the river.

At this hour, when the first rays of sun shone yellow through the seams of his teepee, it was Ka-yip's custom to arise and smoke his first pipeful, but this morning he stayed inside. He watched Bignose get up, make a wry face at the flavor of his tongue, and stagger down to the river for a drink. He came back and hefted the jugs until he found one that contained a heel of liquor. A few swallows of this seemed to be what he needed. With the liquor warming his inside, Bignose made his habitual movement of feeling inside his shirt. He dropped the jug and searched frantically, but was rewarded with nothing except the length of buckskin. He stared at this for a second, and then raised a bellow like a wounded bull buffalo.

"Who stole my buckskin bag?" he roared.

Dakotah sat up and stared blearily. Chiefly because he was the nearest, Bignose reached down, grabbed him by the collar, and shook him like a bulldog shaking a poodle. Dakotah tried to draw his pistol, but Bignose slammed him to the ground so hard it was knocked from his hand.

"Give me that bag you stole!" shouted Bignose.

"I don't know what you're talkin' about," protested Dakotah.

Bignose had his pistol out now, waving at the men who had gathered around. His eyes came to rest on Skinner.

"So you're the one that lifted it!"

"Now, Bignose!" It was Old Dad, still playing his rôle of peacemaker. "Any man in camp might have lifted your nuggets or whatever it was. Put up your gun and let's talk peaceful."

Grudgingly Bignose put up his gun, but he didn't take his

eyes off Skinner. Nothing was said for a while. Rupe came from the cabin, wondering what the excitement was about. Ka-yip shuffled from the teepee and sat down in his accustomed spot by the door flap. The bandits, sensing that the incident was not closed, silently split into the same groups as the day before, three going with Bignose, four with Skinner, leaving Old Dad in the middle.

"Listen, boys," Old Dad pleaded, "this here is bad medicine. No use splittin' up in two camps this way. There's no tellin' who might have got away with it."

Bignose was implacable. "Skinner took it! He. . . ."

"I never took a thing," growled Skinner.

Dakotah snarled: "What you got tied up in this, Welch?"

Old Dad waved them back. "Now hold on. We got no reason to suspect. . . ."

But even as he spoke, Bignose lunged forward, his eyes on the ground by Skinner's foot. A diamond flashed there in the early sun. He snatched it up. Skinner backed away, shaking more jewels from the cuff of his legging with every step. Bignose seemed about to pick up these, too, then he reconsidered and leaped back, his hand streaking for his pistol.

It was war. The morning air rocked with the almost instantaneous explosions of a half dozen guns. Skinner went down from a bullet in the hip, but he rolled to his side and aimed a shot that drove Bignose back on his heels. He fired again, and Bignose toppled. But Skinner's triumph was short, for one of Bignose's followers took aim and downed him for good. Old Dad fled to the protection of a woodpile, but by the time he reached it the battle was over.

Bignose and his followers were wiped out. Skinner and one of his men also lay quiet under the blue-white drift of powder smoke. Another man sat holding a shattered arm and cursing the pain. Rupe had fled behind the cabin, but Ka-yip, inscrutable as always, puffed his morning pipe.

"That settles it," announced Old Dad. "Four men can't rob a steamboat."

Within the hour the surviving bandits saddled and rode away. Ka-yip and Rupe watched them climb the winding trail toward the bench.

"I knew they'd get to fightin' amongst themselves," Rupe insisted. "That's why I didn't try to keep 'em from robbin' the boat."

Ka-yip did not speak. Instead, he reached beneath the slab of sandstone and drew out a gem that flashed blue fire in the sunlight.

Rupe gasped. "Where'd you get that diamond?"

"From the Bignose I took it."

"You mean you stole them rocks off Bignose and cached 'em on Skinner?"

Ka-yip nodded.

"You old fool!" Rupe stamped around and shook his reddish hair indignantly. "Why didn't you keep the rocks and let them fellows rob the boat, or shoot themselves, or whatever they wanted? Them rocks would have put me on easy street. I'd never have had to chop another stick in my life!"

He ranted for a minute or two, and stamped angrily off for the cabin. After a while Wappa-moo scurried up through the grass.

"Good morning, Wappa-moo, my little friend," said Ka-yip. "Did you hear what he would have had me do . . . that chopper of wood? He would have had me take a handful of pretty beads in place of a lifetime of good, strong cigar butts."

★ ★ ★ ★ ★

THAT BUZZARD FROM BRIMSTONE

★ ★ ★ ★ ★

I

Tom Chaddiff awoke and stretched his long, youthful frame. Then he settled back, head against his good center-fire saddle, and watched the bluffs of the Yellowstone move slowly by. Old Ben, the prospector, who had bedded down on the deck of the steamboat the night before, raised up to swat a mosquito.

"Judgin' by the way these 'skeeters has been goin' for me, my blood must taste like sarsaparilly," Ben said. "Whar you headed, cowpoke?"

"Starvation City," Tom Chaddiff stated.

"That robber's roost? Miles City for mine. They just dope your likker and rob you in Miles. They don't shoot a man for his poke like in Starvation City."

"I'm safe. I haven't a poke to drop."

"Busted?" Ben glanced up and down the deck, then he sneaked a heavy buckskin bag from inside his sougan. "Might stake you to some color if you're needin'."

"Thanks, but I got grub money." Chad, as he was commonly called for short, stopped suddenly. He lifted his head from his saddle and stared, then made haste to cover his bare legs. The day before there had been no woman on the boat—but there was one aboard now, and she was coming toward him.

The glare of the early sun was behind her so he couldn't tell much except that she was slim, with shiny blonde hair. As she moved from the sun glare, he saw that she was quite young, no more than twenty. She moved as gracefully as a young deer.

Beautiful! His eyes were so full of her that he scarcely noticed the broad, handsome man who accompanied her. They walked along, looking toward the river, until Chad's bed was only a few yards away.

"Good morning," he felt obliged to say.

The girl took a quick step to one side. "Excuse me! I never supposed anyone. . . ."

Chad grinned and tried to look nonchalant, leaning back on his saddle. "We didn't know there was a woman aboard or we wouldn't have sprawled quite so noticeable. You weren't aboard yesterday."

"I . . . we got on at Fort Union." After saying this she shot a frightened glance at the big man who stood at her side. He didn't look at her. He leaned against the rail with a casual sort of arrogance, looking Chad and Old Ben over as though they were some strange variety of animals. Then he showed his strong teeth in a smile. It was not a friendly grin.

"You appreciate fresh air, I see." The remark was made in a patronizing manner as he rolled his fat cigar from one side of his mouth to the other. He eyed the saddle. "But aren't you a long way from the cattle?"

"Reckon the cattle are some distance away," drawled Chad, "but it seems like I noticed a polecat handy."

Ben snickered. The snicker, as much as the remark, enraged the big man. His face flamed and he took a step away from the rail while his hand swung in toward the ivory-handled revolver at his belt. Chad's hand fell casually toward a lump beneath his sougan. The big man reconsidered. He turned and said something to the girl. Her eyes dropped, and what color was in her cheeks suddenly faded. She turned and followed him without a word, without a backward glance.

"Hope he didn't get a squint at the dust I'm carryin'," Ben growled. Then: "Wonder what an innocent lass like her could be doin' along with him?"

Chad had been wondering the same thing. The episode left him feeling uncomfortable. He slapped a mosquito off the calf of his leg and pulled on his California pants.

"That girl is scared, Ben. It seemed like she was asking for help."

"Worst bullet-swappin' mess I ever did get into was over a woman which I figured was needin' my help," growled Ben.

Chad didn't borrow trouble, either, but he kept thinking about the girl when he went inside for breakfast. The steamboat captain, a heavy, wind-browned man with a halo of snow-white hair, walked in and sat heavily on the bench beside him.

"Well, cowboy, how was it up on deck last night?"

"Fine! I opened my eyes and there was the most beautiful girl I'd ever seen. Who is she?"

The captain looked troubled. "Mary Smith was the name she gave when she got aboard at Fort Union last night. Got on with Jud Goren, that heavy good-looking fellow. They came up from Saint Looie on the *Nellie Mae*."

"Who's this fellow Jud Goren?"

"He used to work for Pierre Ranquette, the Saint Looie fur mogul, but I understand Ranquette sent him packing. Thievery, I heard. Goren's tried lots of things since then."

"Any of them good?"

"Not that I recall." The captain then said unexpectedly: "That Mary Smith gal isn't the kind who should be traveling with him!"

"He's handsome, and women. . . ."

"She's not his wife, nor his sweetheart, if that's what you mean. Between you and me, cowboy, she acted mighty strange when she came aboard this craft. She wouldn't come on at all until Goren snooped around to see who was aboard. On this job I've had considerable practice spotting people on the lope . . . and if she ain't getting away from something, you can call me a muleskinner and spit at me." The captain sawed belligerently at a slice of bacon. "Don't ask me where this Goren fellow fits in, but whatever he's up to is for his own good."

"Where are they headed?"

"Starvation City."

Chad went on deck hoping the girl would come into sight.

Along near mid-morning, he saw Goren talking confidentially with Mapes, a thin, shifty-eyed gambling-house owner from Starvation City who Chad had met the day before. Mapes and Goren seemed to be old friends.

The steamer labored on through silt-heavy water between monotonous gray cutbanks, and stopped about noon at a little wharf where an unkempt French half-breed had a considerable quantity of wood chopped and ready for loading. His cabin, which was also a trading post and liquor establishment, stood a stone's throw away.

Three squaws shuffled aboard with beaded moccasins, pouches, belts, and chokecherries to sell.

In a moment he heard Mary Smith exclaiming the beauty of a pair of beaded moccasins. The squaw jabbered: "Five dollar!" Mary hesitated, then she handed the moccasins back.

"Let me," Chad said.

He held up one finger to the squaw. "One dollar."

The squaw shook her head aggressively. "Five."

Chad finally bought the moccasins for $3. He handed them to the girl and said: "I still paid a dollar too much."

She seemed pleased as a child with the gaudily beaded moccasins. "Thank you, Mister . . . ?"

"Chaddiff, but everyone calls me Chad." Then, casually: "Going far?"

"No. That is. . . ."

"I'm getting off at Starvation City."

He expected her to say Starvation City was her destination, also, but she didn't. She stared at something behind him. He turned to face Goren.

She stammered: "Mister Chaddiff . . . bought me these moccasins."

"I see." Goren drew a gold piece from his vest pocket. There was a cool, off-handed effrontery in his manner,

Chad spoke evenly: "The moccasins were a gift."

Goren flipped the gold piece. It caught the sun as it spun in an arc, struck Chad's shirt front, *jingled* to the deck, rolled away. It was tense for a while, and then Goren decided to smile.

"Sorry, Chaddiff. I guess you meant all right." He extended his hand with affected cordiality. "No hard feelings?"

Chad shook the hand and smiled in return. "None."

"Good. Let's forget anything happened."

Chad wasn't fooled. In spite of the fine words he still saw the calculating hatred in Goren's eyes.

Goren turned to the girl. "Shall we go?"

Her eyes met Chad's for a second as she turned to leave. The pleading, fearful expression he saw in them was like a knife thrusting his vitals.

Chad stood by the rail thinking it over. One of the roustabouts, a great gorilla of a man, who had evidently discovered the wood hawk's liquor supply, weaved aboard, muttered some profane words to the boat in general, and laughed. His eyes finally came to rest on the gold piece. He picked it up and bit it to see if it was genuine.

"Well, damn my britches! Gold right outta heaven!" he whooped.

He pocketed the gold piece and strode happily along the deck, going the same direction taken by Goren and Mary. As he turned from view, he lifted his raucous voice in song. The song suddenly stopped, and a little while later it was followed by excited voices. Chad hurried to see.

He turned the corner by the pilot house and almost stumbled over the roustabout, who was just rising from the floor. Blood trickled from the corner of his mouth and streaked down his jaw bone. Goren stood a few feet away, fists clenched, waiting.

The roustabout faced Goren, rolling his massive muscles. He steadied himself for a moment, then with a full-throated bellow he charged like an enraged Texas steer. Goren calmly weaved back a step, feinted with a left, let the big man's bone-crushing haymaker wrap harmlessly about his shoulder, then he led with a short right hook. It landed on the jaw with a sickening sound—like an axe striking a pumpkin. The roustabout dropped, then painfully pulled himself to hands and knees. Goren waited.

"Get up," he said in his habitual cool voice. "I'll teach you to be civil around a woman."

A crewman muttered: "A person that didn't even know there was a woman around."

"What's that?" Goren demanded.

"Nothing."

"Good! When I need comments, I'll request them."

He waited until the roustabout reeled to his feet, stumbling, hands hanging limply at his sides. Chad stepped forward to stop it, but at the same instant Goren's fist swung. The blow landed flushly on the button, sending the roustabout down heavily, so his weight shook the deck. He was completely unconscious, but Goren leaped forward, swinging a heavy boot to the side of the head. He reached down, dragged the roustabout to his knees, and was aiming another blow when Chad dragged him off.

"Stay out of this!" Goren hissed, his voice thick with fury.

"He's had enough!"

The corners of Goren's mouth twisted in a sneer. The eyes he fastened on Chad were bloodshot with hate. Then he forced himself to smile.

"That big drunk was cursing in front of the lady. Couldn't let that go on."

"Certainly not, but enough's enough."

"Right!" Goren smoothed his coat and wiped his skinned knuckles on a white silk handkerchief. "Enough is enough!"

II

That night, Chad stood by the rail and watched the dark riverbank slide past. In his bed nearby, Old Ben snored.

Chad turned away to wander down the dimly lit companionway. Number 8—that was her cabin. Number 9 beside it belonged to Goren. Lights shone from beneath both doors. He listened. Goren was talking. Chad could hear the deep rumble of his voice for quite a while, but only a few words were distinguishable. Mapes answered. Mapes, who owned the gambling dive in Starvation City. He had a sharp, high-pitched voice that came through the door distinctively:

"Conners doesn't need Sixty-Six Mile badly enough to fight for it, Goren. When he finds out about the girl, he'll have to play our game."

Chad pressed his ear against the door panel, but Goren's answering voice was still a mumble. Now and then Mapes put in a few words, but chiefly he listened. After four or five minutes, Chad gave up and rapped at Mary's cabin. Someone moved inside, but the door did not open.

"Who's there?" she finally asked.

"Me . . . Chad."

A bolt *grated* and the door *squeaked* open a few inches. Her hair was down, and she was wearing a robe of flimsy silk. She must have been getting ready for bed.

"I can't see you," she whispered.

"You're seeing me now." He smiled.

"But Goren . . . he'll. . . ."

"I'm not afraid of Goren."

"But I'm afraid of him. Yes, I'll admit it. But you can't help me. Nobody can help me. And perhaps you wouldn't want to help me if you knew." A sob caught her voice. Whatever she started to say went unspoken. "Oh, sometimes I think it would be better for me if I were dead."

She stepped back into her cabin, and was alone, staring at the blank panels.

He tiptoed back along the companionway, stepped outside, and filled his lungs with the cool evening air.

Chad had a hard time sleeping that night. He kept thinking about Mary. He rolled over and moved the saddle from under his head, but it didn't help him go to sleep. And Old Ben snored and snored.

Chad got up and carried his bed to the other side of the boat. He lay back and stared at the sky. That sky seemed close, just beyond the steamer's tall smokestack, when a man lay like that—like he could almost touch it.

Suddenly he was awake—listening. It seemed as if he'd heard Ben's voice—and a splash. Then he remembered what Mary had said about being better off dead. Not taking time to pull on his boots, he ran to Mary's cabin and called to her. He breathed thanksgiving when she answered: "What do you want?"

He suddenly felt like a fool. "Nothing. Sorry I bothered you."

He wondered if Goren had heard him. He listened, but no sound came from the big man's stateroom. On deck, Chad almost ran into the captain.

"Hello, Chaddiff? What are you doing prowling around at three in the morning without your boots?"

"I thought I heard somebody yell."

"Me, too. Sounded like Old Ben. But you were sleeping

beside him, weren't you?"

"He snored so loud I had to move."

The captain got down a lantern and they hurried on up the deck. Ben's bed was empty. They called his name, but there was no answer.

"Maybe he fell overboard," Chad muttered.

The captain didn't answer right away. He was examining the sougan that was still warm from the old man's body. The captain held his fingers to the lantern. They were streaked red with blood.

"He had a pretty sizable bag of dust on him, didn't he?"

"Yes. He hid it in his blankets every night."

"It's not there now. That man's been murdered and tossed overboard."

"What's wrong down there?" Goren was climbing down from the pilot house.

The captain explained the situation. When he was through, Goren looked Chad over slowly and smiled. "Some jobs are better when a man hasn't got his boots on, hey, Chaddiff?"

Chad whirled on him, but the captain elbowed them apart. "No rough stuff here. I ain't accusing anybody . . . yet. First I'm going to have the boys make a search for the gold."

In another five minutes almost everybody was on deck. Mapes was there, making a great effort at rubbing the sleep from his eyes as he wandered about with half-buttoned shirt. The captain filled the air with orders, and the crew searched everyone and everywhere for the gold. No sign of it.

Finally the China boy ended the hunt by ringing a bell for breakfast. Chad went in with the others, but he noticed that nobody sat near him. He knew the reason—word had gone around that he was guilty of the murder.

The day seemed long. A scorching wind swept in from Wyoming

carrying dust and the odor of prairie fire. He half expected
Goren and Mapes to talk up a necktie party for him, but nothing of the kind materialized. That night passed, and the next
morning. The bluffs then fell away and wide flats stretched on
each side of the river. A good-size stream wandered in from a
remote country of broken, chalk-white hills—and there was a
town scattered haphazardly along the bank.

Starvation City. Now, midway in the first decade of its existence, it was rough and careless and unkempt as might be
expected of a town owing its existence to the chance intersec-
tion of a Texas cattle trail with river navigation. A Sioux village
teeming with papooses and hungry dogs occupied two or three
acres near the docks. Beyond, angling away from the river, was
the strip of deeply pulverized alkali dust that residents dignified
under the name of Main Street. It was lined by two rows of
false-fronted buildings, buildings of log and frame, high and
low, unpainted, warping, and bullet-riddled.

Chad took one look and started up the street loaded down
with saddle and war bag. Finally he saw the sign he'd been
looking for.

Grand Union Hotel
Tie your horse outside
Mrs. P. Murphy, Prop.

He dumped his saddle and war bag and looked around.
Somebody *clattered* in the kitchen. He peeped inside.

Mrs. Murphy wiped her dough-sticky hands on her floor-
length apron and looked him over.

"What d'you want, cowboy?"

"I was looking for a couple of men who promised to meet me
here. They're named Billy Buzzard and the Revener."

"There ain't any sky pilots shook down here, far as I know.
But we might have some buzzards."

"They'll be along in a day or so. Can you fix me up with a bed?"

"Might sleep you with that drummer. Two dollars . . . in advance."

He paid the $2 and carried his saddle and war bag upstairs. Then he wandered back along the street looking over the camp. Mapes owned a place here—the Gilded Cage Opera. It wasn't hard to find. A combination saloon, hurdy-gurdy, gambling house, and theater. He went inside. There was Mapes himself, standing behind the bar. He didn't look up.

Chad placed a few bets at the faro spread. When he turned back toward the bar, Mapes was gone. It made Chad wonder. He rolled a cigarette, smoked it, flipped the butt away, and *clomped* toward the door. He drew up quite suddenly, hand falling to the butt of his Colt six-gun. Mapes, Goren, and a couple of strangers were hurrying up the sidewalk. One of the strangers, a squat, stern-faced man, spoke: "You Chaddiff that just got off the boat?"

"That's right."

"I'm Dod Britt, sheriff, and you're under arrest." Britt's hands hovered near his six-guns, but he made no move to draw.

"What am I being arrested for?"

"You know well enough, cowboy."

The other stranger, a florid, flabby man dressed in a soup-stained black suit, now spoke up: "You, sir, are charged with the murder and robbery of one Benjamin Robbins, alias Old Ben, a capital offense under the laws of the fair and prosperous Territory of Montana."

"And who are you?" Chad asked.

"I, sir, am Judge Augustus Hule, commissioner and justice of the peace."

Chad turned on Goren. "So this is your game! You think you can saddle me with a crime you committed yourself."

Goren's lips twisted into a smug smile. "It's just that I don't like to see killers of your stamp loose in the same town with me, that's all."

"I suppose you own the so-called court here in Starvation City."

"I resent the implication of those words, sir!" Judge Hule spluttered, spitting a fragment of sodden cigar. "My court, sir, is renowned for justice from one end of the Yellowstone to the other."

"Would it be offending the dignity of Your Honor to inquire just what proof you have against me?"

The judge gnawed this over for a while. Evidently no proof had yet been presented. "That, sir, will no doubt evolve during the trial."

"We have proof enough," the sheriff insisted. "Goren was in the pilot house playin' cribbage when the murder took place. He practically seen you in the act."

Goren cut in: "We'd better have a look for the old man's gold."

Britt took Chad's gun. "Where's your war bag?" he asked.

"Mother Murphy's."

They climbed the stairs to the big front bedroom. Chad's war bag lay on the bed where he had left it. He glanced at the knot. It didn't appear to have been tampered with. He breathed easier then.

The sheriff rummaged through without having much luck. Then he drew out a heavy buckskin sock. It was Old Ben's, all right, although now only a third filled.

"There's his initials burned in the buckskin." Goren smiled. "That ought to cinch it."

Yes, that cinched it! Chad now saw that he didn't have a chance. Any frontier court would hang him on this kind of evidence. He must act now. But the sheriff had taken his gun.

No chance to fight. He glanced at the window. Two beds stood in the way. The sheriff was still pawing in the war bag. Goren was hefting the buckskin sack. Judge Hule stood right behind Chad, and Mapes behind the judge.

Chad casually rammed Judge Hule. The unexpected force of it sent him reeling against Mapes. A reflex motion brought the gun from Mapes's holster, but it tangled in the judge's suit. Chad flung them both from his path and made the door at a leap. He saw Mother Murphy then, but it was too late. She was halfway up the stairs. He tripped and sprawled headlong to the bottom. He tried to rise, but the room spun. He felt as hopeless as the ball in a roulette wheel.

The next thing he knew, Sheriff Britt was clamping his wrists in handcuffs.

"That ought to hold you, Mister Killer," the lawman growled.

Judge Hule came puffing down, disheveled, eyes bloodshot with rage, the cigar crushed and resembling a mouthful of spinach.

"This means hanging," he wheezed. "Hanging, I repeat, or I'm not judge of the court of Starvation City."

III

It was afternoon, and the white-hot sun beat down on the bleached buildings of Starvation City as two riders dropped down from the rimrock country and paused for a while to look over the town. The shorter of them, a gray-whiskered man with shrewd blue eyes, hooked one knee over the pommel of his low-shelled saddle, and settled dust with a spurt of tobacco juice.

"Well, Revener, thar she be. Starvation City, the fair jewel of the Yellastone. Surprisin' how civilization keeps creepin' in on a country. Last time I seen her she had one shanty and three tepees. That was in the summer of 'Seventy-Five or 'Seventy-Six."

"Must have been the year 'Seventy-Six," croaked his tall partner—the Revener. "In 'Seventy-Five you sojourned in that Oregon jail."

"So I did. Lucky I have you along to keep cases on me. Facts like them will come in handy when you write my autobiography."

"Biography," corrected the Revener. "Autobiography. That's Latin meanin' a biography somebody ought to write. All you know is what's inside that Bible of your'n. You ain't wide-read. Should be you'd have better judgment than to argue with a man which was snowed in for five solid months with Doctor Heppner's *Almanac* and a complete set o' Shakespeare."

The Revener looked pityingly down on his companion, then he sighed and slumped still farther in his saddle, an act that made him appear even more gangling than he actually was— and the Revener was a gangling man. He was long and loose, bony as a pilgrim longhorn after four months on an iced range. Dressed in decrepit cotton pants, flapping swallow-tailed coat, and ancient black sombrero, he resembled a poorly upholstered scarecrow.

"I've read a pack of things besides the Bible in my time," he was moved to say.

"Tracts and such." Billy Buzzard sat proudly upright, palms resting on the butts of his two six-guns, and spat with fine accuracy between the perked-up ears of his bronco. "But Shakespeare! 'Now is the very witching time of night, when. . . .' "

"It's not night," interposed the Revener. "It's afternoon, and we're two days late meetin' Chad in yonder Starvation City. Like's not he's up and gone prospecting without us."

They rode through town, reining in before the largest establishment, a two-story affair, its proud false front emblazoned with a sign reading: *Gilded Cage Opera*. The Revener followed Billy Buzzard through the swinging doors. Billy dragged his spurs to the bar, and asked: "Wet your dusty throat, Revener?"

"I don't mind."

The bartender set out a bottle and two glasses. Billy poured his drink, but not the Revener, who said: "Water for me."

The bartender started to complain, but there was something in Billy Buzzard's eyes that made him change his mind. He slid the glass of water over to the Revener.

"Cowboy hereabouts named Chaddiff?" Billy asked.

The bartender straightened up and shot a hurried glance at a dapper little man who lolled a few steps away.

"He's in town. For permanent by what I understand."

"What d'you mean by that?"

"I mean he's in the lock-up waitin' to get hung."

Billy Buzzard did not change expression. He pretended to be interested in catching a fly that had rested on the neck of the bottle. "And when's this projected hangin' due to take place?"

"Tomorrow at sunup."

"The charge?"

"Robbery and murder. He knocked off a prospector called Old Ben for his poke of dust."

"Old Ben! Seems like I recollect him from over Deadwood way. But you're tangled in your picket rope if you think Chad knocked anybody over for his poke. Chad's a fightin' man, but he's honest as I am."

"Heap more honest," added the Revener.

"Just what proof they got?" asked Billy.

"Proof aplenty, I guess. Mapes here was on the boat. He says Chaddiff is sure enough guilty."

"Well, you tell your Mapes that he's a ring-tailed liar."

Billy's voice was subdued and dead level, but there was something about it that carried to every corner of the room.

The drone of voices and the chip *rattle* instantly ceased.

Mapes drew up, frozen-faced, tense. Billy Buzzard was loose-jointed and cool as ever, but he moved back a few inches from the bar. He couldn't see Mapes's hands, but a flicker of the eyes and a little droop of the shoulders flashed its message. Billy wheeled to one side. His right-hand Colt seemed to leap to his hand.

But the Revener was also in action. He elbowed Billy off balance, and, with a continuing motion, reached far across the bar to clip Mapes with the whiskey bottle. Billy's gun roared, but the bullet, flying wild, planted a spider web of cracks in the mirror. Mapes's gun slipped from his fingers and he went face forward to the floor. The bartender reached for something, then stopped.

"Keep your hands innocent, my good man," the Revener advised. "I've flung these things before."

Billy spluttered: "You idjit! What did you want to horn in for? I had him outdrawed, didn't I? One of these days you're gonna run into a flock of lead elbowing in on my personal arguments."

"And one of these days you're going to get your neck tangled in a rope I can't talk you out of. Put your pistol away and let's get out of this deadfall."

The jail, sheriff's office, and courtroom occupied a squat building of thick cottonwood logs in a rubbish-littered spot back of Main Street. When Billy Buzzard and the Revener approached, its screenless door stood open and the white afternoon sun beat in on the tobacco-littered floor. Inside someone was snoring. Cards *slap-slapped* on a table.

Billy stood in the door while his eyes became accustomed to the shadowy interior. A freckled, placid-faced man wearing a deputy's badge looked up from his solitaire game with suspicion in his eyes. The snores came from a dinky side room. Billy extended his hand and said: "Howdy, deppity. I'm William

Tecumseh Boussard from Brimstone, Arizony. The long-geared gent to my rear is the Revener. Revener bein' a polite term for sky-pilot."

They shook hands. "My name's Tom Cotton," said the deputy. "What's you gents' pleasure?"

"We're here for the purpose of visitin' with one Chad Chaddiff."

Deputy rubbed his chin. *"Hmm,"* he pondered.

"Is that an unusual request?"

"Ordinarily, no. But you see we're hangin' Chaddiff at sunup, and that makes him sort of a special prisoner. The sheriff left orders he wasn't to be visited by nobody."

Billy Buzzard looked amazed. "You mean you're holdin' him incommunicado?" When this won nothing but a startled look from Cotton, Billy went on: "You realize you can't hold a prisoner incommunicado without a writ of *corpus delicti*?"

Deputy Cotton wiped away some perspiration with his shirt sleeve. "I ain't much up on law stuff," he admitted. "I'm just a deppity, but Judge Hule's right here. Judge! Hey, Judge!"

The snoring broke with a couple of quick snorts, and Judge Hule came from an adjoining room looking red-eyed and evil-tempered.

"What do you want?"

"This man wants to know some things about where's our corpus delicti?"

"Hmm, well. . . ." The judge pompously cleared his throat. "You're referring to the Chaddiff case, no doubt?"

"No doubt," answered Billy Buzzard.

"Certainly. Now about the *corpus delicti* . . . we haven't one for the simple reason that Chaddiff threw it overboard."

"Somebody see him?"

"Do you suggest that my court condemned a man to the gallows, to the supreme penalty, sir, without . . . ?"

"Don't bust your buttons, Judge. I know my rights. I've read a heap o' law in my time, ain't I, Revener?"

"Could be," intoned the Revener.

"Yep, a pack o' law. Blackstone . . . he's just Old Scratch to me. Common law and the revised stat-choots, too. As a lawyer I ask, when was the trial held?"

"Yesterday," answered Judge Hule nervously.

"Yesterday! And the hangin's tomorrow at sunup? Ain't that rushin' justice along?"

Judge Hule struck a match and almost burned his bulbous nose before he noticed that there was no cigar in his mouth. He cursed and threw the match away.

"There was no request for an appeal, no extenuating. . . ."

"Thar's a request for an appeal now, and I'm makin' it."

The judge hemmed around, trying to figure a way out of his dilemma. "This is highly irregular. Well, I'll give him a stay of execution until Friday morning. We have few facilities for holding prisoners here in Starvation City, and any further delay would prove embarrassing. Yes, most embarrassing."

The judge's throat had become husky, so he headed across to the rear door of a saloon. With considerable deference, Deputy Cotton then showed them down a short corridor to a closed door. He rapped. An eye appeared at a slot.

"It's all right," said Cotton.

A gruff voice answered: "Tell 'em to leave their guns back in the office!"

Cotton took Billy's guns away.

"You take a heap o' precautions here," Billy observed.

"You bet! We can't afford to take chances. We got it pretty level that some buzzard or other was comin' up from the Wyoming country to pull a rescue, and from what we hear he's a rip-roaring terror." Cotton chuckled. "Must admit, I thought mebby you was him . . . that is, before I seen you was a sure-enough lawyer."

The bolt now *grated* and the door *creaked* open. A truculent, dull-looking fellow looked them up and down. Then he sat back in his chair once more with his sawed-off shotgun across his knees.

"His name is Pennington," said Cotton. Pennington might have been deaf for all the acknowledgment he gave this introduction.

"Visitors for you, Chaddiff," Cotton said through the slot in a cell door.

Billy looked over his shoulder, "Your name Chaddiff?" he demanded, heading off Chad's greeting. "I'm William Tecumseh Boussard, attorney-at-the-bar."

After Cotton was gone and the hand shakings and back-slappings were completed, Chad explained events since getting on the steamer.

Billy chuckled. "It was the gal. You made a play for Goren's gal, and now he wants to get you out of. . . ."

"She's not his girl! He has her with him for some reason . . . a reason I tried to find out but couldn't. And that's why he wants to get me out of the way . . . so I won't find out."

The Revener, long silent, now exploded with accumulated indignation: "You say those hounds o' Satan are forcing an innocent gal to play party to some low-down scheme? Blast their hides! Set me at 'em. I'll strangle 'em with my two hands. . . ."

"Now, Revener," temporized Billy. "Recollect what the Good Book says."

"I know plenty well what it says."

"And, anyhow, you already bashed one of 'em with a whiskey bottle. But back to this gal . . . where is she now?"

"I don't know. The last I saw of her she was getting off the boat yesterday."

★ ★ ★ ★ ★

After leaving the cell, Billy Buzzard was thoughtful.

"What do you aim?" the Revener finally asked.

"I'd've had him out already and been miles into the badlands if it hadn't been for you," Billy shot back petulantly.

"What have I done now?" wailed the Revener.

"Nothin'. Nothin' at all. It's just that you impede me. Let me follow my own inclinations and I'd've throwed my hide-out Derringer on that baboon they got for a guard, opened the door, locked him and Cotton in the cell. or maybe I'd've shot 'em, I don't know. Then I'd. . . ."

"Then you'd have had the whole country on your trail with the result you and Chad would both be dangling from a cotton-wood inside a week. Anyhow," the Revener added placidly, "left to your own inclinations you'd have got yourself hung many years ago and hence wouldn't have been here anyhow."

"Sure, do a man a favor and then throw it up to him every day for eight years. Nag, nag, nag! Worse'n a unbeat woman. Why don't you go back to Missoury and leave me alone?"

"Don't dast. You're my prize convert, Buzzard, and I intend to ride herd on you. If I went back to Missouri, you'd be back to robbin' stagecoaches inside a month."

Billy nudged the Revener to silence. He stepped quickly into the rear of a harness shop, the Revener close behind. Two men were walking toward the jail. One, whose hat was worn rakishly because of a bump along his head, was Mapes. The other man was broad, handsome, and hard-eyed.

"Must be Goren," said the Revener. He squinted and rubbed his long jaw bone thoughtfully the way he always did when conjuring memories from away back. "Does he sort of remind you of somebody?"

"Yes, now you mention it," Billy responded sourly. "Reminds me of a rattlesnake I caught stealin' eggs down in Yuma."

"Serious, though . . . I've seen him before some place. Had something to do with a fence. Barbed wire. I can just see him standing there by a high gate . . . I got it! Sweetwater in Kansas! Recollect? Bunch of varmints bought up nesters' holdings along the Sweetwater and fenced it off, knowing trail herds couldn't travel clear from Taylor's to Willow River without water. Hired those shootin' McCarney boys to gun for them."

Billy slapped his leg. "By jingoes, he's the one. That was four years ago. He was in with Three-Gun Guffy, who was later rope-stretched over in Trail City."

"Wonder what he's doing up here . . . and with a girl?"

They inquired inside. The harness maker had seen no one who answered Mary's description. They asked all along the street. Starvation City had not seen her, and the arrival of a beautiful girl was not the sort of thing Starvation City usually overlooked. They ended up near the cracker barrel in Solly Thompson's General Store. Billy was munching one of the salty tidbits when a squaw shuffled in. After much grunting and gesturing, she bought a bar of scented toilet soap.

"That squaw there never washed in her whole life. What's she buyin' fancy soap for?" marveled Billy. He turned to Solly, the storekeeper. "Who's the squaw?"

"Gopher Girl. Belongs to Neils Forster."

"She in the habit of buyin' soap?"

"Can't tell what an Injun will buy. Maybe she eats it."

"Who's this Neils Forster?"

"Rancher. Got a little spread five or six miles up the Squawknife. First ranch you come to."

"This Forster's a pretty good friend of Goren and Mapes, ain't he?"

"Why, yes, he seems to be."

Billy and the Revener rode to Forster's ranch. It was like every other two-bit spread in the territory—a long log house with a pole-and-dirt roof, straggling pole corrals, a flat-roofed shed, the abandoned remains of a wagon.

A girl came to the door of the house and shaded her eyes as they rode up. She was blonde and possessed a peculiarly fragile beauty. Billy doffed his battered hat with a fine flourish.

"Miss Smith, I believe?"

She looked surprised. "Why . . . yes."

"Boussard is the name. William Tecumseh Boussard, though I'm known in song and story as plain Billy Buzzard. This gent with me which resembles a p'fessional pallbearer is none other than the Revener."

"I'm glad to know you," she faltered.

"We wanted to see you on account of Chad."

"Chad . . . oh, yes!" They noticed that she colored slightly. "How is Mister Chaddiff?"

"Cheerful as could be expected in a man sentenced to hang Friday mornin'."

Her face whitened. "Hang?"

"Yes, ma'am."

"But why? For what?"

"For the murder of Old Ben."

"Why, that's ridiculous! What proof could they have?"

"Proof aplenty. Mapes and Goren gave all the testimony that was needed, and to cinch it somebody planted Ben's poke in Chad's war bag."

After a moment of tight-lipped silence, she asked: "Why did you come to me?"

"We figured you could help us. You see, it was on account of you that Goren decided to get Chad out of the way. Chad found out you weren't traveling with Goren because you wanted to."

"Perhaps Mister Goren is a relative of mine."

"And perhaps he ain't. Now you quit play-actin' and tell us

182

what's the trouble. Chances are we could help you."

"No. Please . . . nobody can help me." She stood there, looking up with tears glistening in her eyes. Then she turned and ran in great haste back inside the house.

"Poor little chicken," the Revener mourned as they headed back toward Starvation City. "Just a chicken that got mixed up with the hawks."

"Yep, but did you ever see what happens to the hawks when a buzzard starts roostin' amongst 'em?" Billy inquired.

IV

The following afternoon, Goren, Mapes, and a tall, hard-faced cattleman paused in front of Solly Thompson's General Store. The tall cattleman was Jim Delling, minority partner of Brent Conners in the big Diamond C cattle spread.

"Brent Conners is your partner, Delling," Goren was saying. "It won't hurt to try to convince him he can get along without water from Sixty-Six Mile."

"It won't help," Delling answered doggedly. "Brent Conners didn't get to be the biggest cattleman in the territory being that kind of a fool."

"He's right," Mapes put in. "Conners will hang onto it tighter than ever now with all this railroad talk."

"I'll make a fool of Conners before I'm finished," Goren insisted. "He'll come to time quick enough when he finds out about the girl. Wasn't she a windfall, though? I can use her to get Conners's property and to even that overdue account with Ranquette, too."

The three wandered on. Billy Buzzard took a deep breath and appeared from behind the cracker barrel. He helped himself to a sample, and munched thoughtfully.

"Solly, who is Ranquette?"

"Only Ranquette I recollect is Pierre, the big fur man at Saint Looie."

"Pierre Ranquette. *Hmm.*" Billy helped himself to another cracker. "Nothin' to these things, is there? Mostly holes. Must have put too much sody in 'em."

"Sorry you don't like my crackers," Solly grumbled.

Billy munched. "Does Ranquette have a family? Say a gal of about twenty?"

"Not him. A dashin' Frenchie, that Ranquette, but he's never been churched with a woman."

"How about Brent Conners?"

"Big cattleman. Fifty or so. Bachelor. Nothin' unusual about that. You're usually either a bachelor or a squawman in Montana."

"Strange thing. Very strange, indeed." Billy, still mumbling, put four or five crackers into his pocket and left the store. Solly shrugged and curled up for a *siesta* on the blanket counter.

Billy found the Revener at Mother Murphy's.

"Three new elements have entered the mixture, my sky-pilot friend . . . elements known as Ranquette, Conners, and the Sixty-Six Mile spring."

"Talk straight, Buzzard."

"Meanin' that my long ears have come in handy. I just found out that Goren is after two birds with one stone. The birds are Ranquette and Conners. The stone is little Mary Smith. . . ."

About sundown that evening, the second steamboat of the week churned the water to Starvation City's dock. It was the *Black Hawk,* a packet from St. Louis. Four passengers came ashore. Two were women—women with mascaraed eyes and kalsomined faces, destined to swell the total of pulchritude at the Gilded Cage. Another was a cattleman, and the last was a thin, jumpy, young man who seemed to be looking for somebody.

After hesitating a while, he started up the street, lugging a floppy carpetbag, and after some hesitation turned in at Mother Murphy's. In half an hour he came out again.

Billy went inside and inquired of Mother Murphy.

"Who's the young pilgrim?"

"Didn't ask. But you galoots got something in common with him."

"How's that?"

"Remember you was here yesterday inquirin' about a blonde gal? Now he's doing it."

Billy whistled. "C'mon, Revener, before the century plants take root on us. That lad is likely to prove right interestin'."

During the day, the 2R and Shanahan outfits had driven trail herds across the Yellowstone, and now the sidewalks and saloons of the camp were teeming with cowpunchers who hankered after a taste of town life. When Billy and the Revener came out of Mother Murphy's, the air was still foggy from the passage of galloping horses.

Billy and the Revener walked along, inquiring as they went. A barber whose chair was in the front of Long William's Saloon reported seeing someone of the newcomer's description entering the Gilded Cage.

So Billy and the Revener ambled over, mingling as inconspicuously as possible among some 2R cowpunchers. The young stranger didn't appear to be around. Somebody tapped Billy's elbow. It was the bouncer, a raw-boned, unwashed gunslinger known as Long-Haired Jess.

"Don't try none o' your fandangos in here," he warned.

Billy spun on him, and Long-Haired Jess retreated a step, his hand close to the double-barreled pistol at his belt.

"I ain't hankerin' for trouble, Buzzard, but I don't mind sayin' you and your sky-pilot pard are about as welcome around here as two Injuns with the smallpox. So I ask you in a nice, peaceful way to take your custom somewheres else."

"And if we don't?"

"Then we'll see whether I'm as good at dodgin' Forty-Five slugs as you are wigglin' around the buckshot I got my old pistol loaded with."

Billy Buzzard's eyes were cold as granite, but the Revener collared him. "Careful, Billy, this yahoo is taking no chances. He has a couple of his gun hands planted."

Long-Haired Jess showed his tobacco-stained teeth in a grin. "Yep! We take precautions."

Billy considered this situation. "Never did like to hang out where I wasn't welcome," he admitted, trying to watch both ways from the corners of his eyes. "And this ain't my idea of genteel surroundings, anyhow. We came in here lookin' for a friend."

"Who is he?"

"Young pilgrim. A skinny, pale sort of critter."

Jess shot a quick glance in the direction of the rear stairs. "He ain't been here."

"Not upstairs by any freak of circumstance?"

"I said he warn't here."

"Uhn-huh. Well, if he ain't, he ain't." He knew Jess was lying, but there was no point in arguing. Still, something prompted him to stick around. He stuffed one cheek with cut plug, and chewed thoughtfully for a while. "You're an old buffalo hunter, ain't you, Jess?"

"What's that got to do with it?" Jess brayed impatiently. "I answered your question about the tenderfoot, now. . . ."

A sudden *clump* and *clatter* up above made Jess stop. The report of a small-caliber gun came clearly. Someone was running. A man cried out and another cursed. Feet *thumped* down an outside stairway. Billy elbowed Jess out of his way and ran for the rear door to see what was going on. Jess was off balance for a couple of seconds, then cursed and went for his double-barreled pistol. He drew it, but the Revener connected with a long, limber kick that knocked the weapon from his hand and sent it skittering beneath the feet of the press of cowpunchers at the bar.

The Revener stooped low, melting into the crowd that was now milling from the excitement. Jess roared and cursed. Someone threw a whiskey bottle. "Yuh can't talk thataway to a Texan!" shouted a big cowboy. There was a great whooping and yelling.

A chair splintered. "Hunt your holes, you Yallerstone rats!" And the fight was on. Everyone took a swing at somebody. The Revener, whose six feet five made him too attractive a target, stayed on hands and knees. When he had the chance, he slipped out the back door.

It was dark in the alley. The sounds of battle seemed distant now that the door was closed. He edged along through the dark. "Billy," he called in a quiet voice.

Someone moved quite close to him. He spun for cover instinctively. A streak of flame leaped at him. It was so close he could feel the sting of burning powder.

Without quite knowing how he got there, the Revener found himself inside an icehouse. The sawdust was spongy and damp beneath his feet. He was quiet until a shuffle of boots in the alley told him that the bushwhacker had moved on.

"Revener?"

The voice came from right beside him. It was Billy Buzzard.

"It's me. Where you, Billy?"

"By the wall. The young critter's with me. He's dead."

The Revener felt along in the dark. He put an ear to the young fellow's breast, then he assumed a kneeling posture and said the Lord's Prayer.

"Who shot him, Billy?" he asked when he was through.

"Mapes, Goren . . . who else could it be? I saw him stagger down the stairs and in here. He was still alive when I found him. He kept mumblin' somethin' about Ranquette. Ranquette . . . he's the Saint Looie fur man, you recollect. And he says . . . 'Tell Sis I . . . ,' and that was the end of it. He just up and died."

"Strange medicine the way this Ranquette fellow keeps cropping up," pondered the Revener. "I don't heap savvy it. One thing seems certain. This chap's Mary Smith's brother."

"You ride out and break the news, Revener. Such things're in a preacher's line. I'll get me over and report this business to the sheriff. If he and the judge are honest as they claim to be, our friend Mapes may have to do some wigglin' to keep a rope from his neck."

Billy couldn't find the sheriff. He watched for a while from the Elk Saloon. Then he ambled out onto the street. He drew up quite suddenly when a hard object was rammed against his spine. He heard the voice of Long-Haired Jess.

"Keep peaceful, Buzzard, and lift them hands. It wouldn't make me weep much if I had to pull this trigger."

The two gun-toters came up, one on either side. They relieved Billy of his two six-guns and felt him over until they found his hide-out Derringer.

"We're just dehorning you for your own protection," Jess explained. "It ain't the plan to shoot you . . . not yet."

Billy went peacefully enough. They took him across heaps of ashes, bottles, and assorted rubbish to the rear of a livery stable. Jess spoke to somebody inside, and in a minute or two a man led out four saddle horses. Billy's was a big-footed nag that couldn't outrun a Jersey cow, but even so Jess kept the horse on a lead rope.

They took the trail up the Squawknife until the last houses of

Starvation City were left behind, then they headed over the bluffs and on across the vast prairie toward the northwest. A steady pace, hour after hour. Sunrise and the Yellowstone were far behind. At mid-morning they reached a broken country of deep coulées and wind-carved sandstone. It was a land of greasewood and cactus and rattlesnakes. In the distance were scattering clumps of box elder and an occasional solitary cottonwood. The horses perked up and footed it a little faster. They had scented water.

The water stood in little pools at the bottom on a drying creekbed. Close by stood a one-room cabin of knotty cottonwood logs. Abandoned. Its door hung wearily on leather hinges, its dirt roof sagged in decay.

"This is her, Buzzard," Jess announced, spitting in the direction of the log cabin. "The end of the line for you."

"Seems like a long way to take a man just to shoot him," Billy remarked.

"It's right on our way or we wouldn't have. Anyhow, we ain't had orders to shoot you . . . not yet."

"When will you get them orders?"

"Might be soon, or it might be late. Mebby, if you play the game, not at all. Wouldn't be surprised if the boss should want a little conflab with you tonight."

Jess fried doughgods and bacon. They ate. Billy had no opportunity to escape. His legs were roped to a pole that supported a bunk. The man played red dog. Evening, and Jess lit a candle. Billy knew it was too late now. The fastest horse in the territory could not carry him to town before sunrise in time to save Chad from hanging.

V

In the meantime, Chad sat on the edge of his bunk in the Starvation City jail. The Revener had been to see him several times that day, at first hopeful, then less so, and finally he wanted Chad to join him in prayer. That told the story well enough. Barring a miracle, Chad's number was up.

He rolled a cigarette and smoked thoughtfully. Someone galloped up beside the jail. He tried to see from the little window. Footsteps—quick, light footsteps. Like a woman's. The door to the sheriff's office opened and closed. Five minutes passed. He smoked the cigarette down to his fingers, snapped it into corner, rolled another. He almost jumped out of his Texas boots when Sheriff Britt shouted in to the guard: "Bring Chaddiff out to the office."

Chad blinked in the bright light of the office before he saw who was standing there. Mary! She was staring at him, her underlip clenched tightly in her teeth, her hands clutching the back of a chair. Judge Hule sat behind his desk, sober for a change. Sheriff Britt and Deputy Cotton were also in the room.

The judge cleared his throat several times. "Miss Smith has some new evidence in your case, Chaddiff."

She spoke in a rapid voice: "I came to tell you that if you hang Chad . . . Mister Chaddiff . . . for that murder, you're hanging an innocent man. I know he's innocent. He isn't the kind who would rob or murder."

"My dear young lady," boomed the judge, "what you have said seems to be only in the manner of a personal opinion. I'm afraid such opinions haven't a place in law. Now, if you have any new evidence to offer, real evidence. . . ."

"I said I know he's innocent!" Her voice, revealing her tension, raised a little.

"Now hold on, Miss Smith. The captain of the steamboat said you were in your cabin at the time of the murder. You went to bed about dark, and you were in your cabin until ten minutes after the murder was discovered. Is that true, or isn't it?"

"That's true." Her head was held high, and she looked the

judge directly in the eye.

"Then how do you know who's guilty of . . . ?"

"Because Chad was in my cabin at the time the murder was committed!"

For a moment Chad wondered if he had heard correctly. He felt unsteady, as if the floor were moving beneath his feet. Judge Hule stood up, then as suddenly sat back down.

"He was in . . . your . . . cabin?"

"Yes. We both heard Old Ben's cry and the splash when he was thrown overboard."

The judge turned to Chad: "Is that true?"

Chad started to answer, but the girl's voice rose to cut him off. "There's no need asking him. He'll deny it. What else could a gentleman do?"

"Of course I'll deny it!" Chad finally made himself heard, but he could tell that nobody believed him. "I didn't murder Old Ben and I wasn't in this girl's cabin, either."

"My word should be all that is necessary," she announced firmly. "He was there, and I'll sign a statement saying so."

Judge Hule cleared his throat. "You don't need to sign anything, miss. We've got witnesses. That satisfies the law, and you're a free man, Chaddiff. And man to man, I admire you for keeping your mouth shut when you were just three jumps away from the noose. . . ."

Chad wasn't listening. He started for the girl, but she turned and fled through the door. He followed in time to see her leap onto her horse and go galloping away. A saddled horse that belonged to Deputy Cotton was tied at the rack. Chad swung into the saddle and was after her.

After a two-mile chase up the Squawknife he caught her.

"What do you want?" There seemed to be a sob in her voice. "Why can't you just leave me alone? Why can't everybody leave me alone?"

"But Mary. . . ."

"I couldn't let them hang you, that's why I lied! Not when I was the cause. I'd have done the same for anybody."

He seized her horse's bridle. "I haven't forgotten that night back on the boat."

"Please, Chad. I'm sorry if I gave you the wrong impression. . . ."

"You didn't!" His voice rang with a sudden intensity of emotion. Chad was usually abashed around women, but now he forgot himself. He discovered that his tongue was saying things that had been lying in the back of his mind and heretofore scarcely admitted to himself. "You do care for me. I've known it ever since that night aboard the boat. There's no use of your claiming otherwise. Let's be honest with each other. Mary, I'm in love with you. You're the only girl I've ever felt this way about. I've loved you ever since the. . . ."

"Chad, don't. Don't talk that way. You don't know about . . . about my past."

"I don't care about your past."

"Chad. . . ." It seemed a long time that she sat there, looking at him, before she completed her sentence. "Chad . . . I'm another man's wife."

It was like a blow between his eyes. He felt as if he should say something, but there was nothing for him to say.

She started to speak then, in a rapid voice, trying to tell her story as quickly as possible: "Ranquette. You've heard the name. According to the law he's my husband. For years he wanted to marry me, ever since I was a little girl. But I hated him. I hated him and I was afraid of him. But then my brother entered the picture. He was irresponsible. He gambled. He drank. He worked for Ranquette and embezzled money . . . a great deal of money. It made no difference that Ranquette had made it easy for him to take the money. He would have sent my brother to prison anyway. It would have killed my mother, Chad. So I married Ranquette. As soon as the ceremony was over, I went to my room, sneaked from the window, and caught a steamboat. It was bound for Montana Territory where my father lived. He and Mother separated when I was a little girl. Then Goren boarded the boat. He knew why I was running away. I had to do as he said or he'd notify Ranquette. Even though he was using me as a tool to rob my father, there was nothing I could do. You see why I couldn't let you help me. You see why there can never be anything between us. . . ."

Suddenly she twisted her horse away and lashed with the quirt end of her bridle. The hoofs *thundered* off along the trail, leaving him there, staring dully after her.

She disappeared around a clump of buffalo berry bushes. He watched, expecting her to reappear further up the Squawknife. Several minutes passed, but he saw no more of her. Wondering, his eyes roved the hillsides. Finally he glimpsed her riding up a brushy draw. She was briefly silhouetted on the evening skyline. She must be headed for the north country—for the vast Brent Conners range.

Chad turned to follow. His horse slid down a steep bank, *splashed* through the muddy stream. Then he pulled up to listen. Horses—approaching from up the Squawknife. A clump of bushes gave concealment while he waited. In a moment two riders came into sight. One was Goren, the other was a hunched graying man in flapping, sun-bleached clothing. When they were abreast of him, Goren bore back on his bridle with a brutal twist of his arm that sent the horse pawing to its haunches. Blood from the beast's mouth mixed with the foam that strung down from the bit. The elder man got stopped a few rods farther on and came back. Goren pointed to the ground.

"Those are fresh tracks, Neils. She must have headed across the stream right here. What do you suppose she has in mind?

By the devil, if I thought she was headed for Brent Conners . . . !"

The gray man climbed down to examine the tracks more closely. "Hold on, Goren."

"Hold on, hell! I'm going to run down that girl. And if I can't run her down, I'll drop her with my Thirty-Thirty. I'll kill her just like I'll kill that stubborn Brent Conners. I'm through cat-footing it on this deal. . . ."

"But these aren't her tracks." The gray-haired man was lying and doing a good job of it. "She grabbed that big bay gelding out in the corral. He was steel-shod. This hoss ain't even got steel shoes. Looks like he'd been shod with rawhide. Here's her tracks yonder. And they're headed for town. On the long lope, too, by the looks."

Chad waited until they were out of sight, then he pointed his horse up the brushy coulée. Once out of the valley of the Squawknife he stopped to look across the wide prairie.

It was several minutes before he caught sight of the girl emerging from a dry wash. She was two or three miles away, riding hard.

Back in the cabin, Long-Haired Jess hurled his cards down with a force that made the candle flame dance. He cursed some mighty oaths.

"Never did see such cyards! I'll never play this game of red dog again as long as I live." He fumbled in his pocket and drew out his last three gold pieces. "Gimme some bettin' money, Hodson."

Billy Buzzard was still roped to the bunk. No chance to escape, and he realized it was too late for escape anyway. Too late to save Chad. The red dog game went on. Luck changed presently for Jess and he was in better humor. Slick lifted his hand for silence. They all listened.

"Hosses," Slick muttered.

Hodson jumped up and got his Winchester that was leaning near the door. Jess blew out the candle.

It seemed a long while that they waited in the dark. Hoofs *clattered* over some stones down in the creekbed. Then a voice: "Hey, up there!"

"It's the boss," Jess said in a relieved tone. Billy could hear a couple of guns *click* as the hammers were lowered. "He's here a heap earlier than I expected. Wonder what's up." Then he bellowed: "Waal, come on in! We got your guest here, if you aim to conflab with him."

Jess whipped a match to flame on the seat of his sourdough pants and lit the candle. Hodson put back the Winchester. Goren then strode through the doorway. He was followed by a gray-haired man who Billy had never seen before.

Goren seemed to be in a hurry. He motioned at Billy, and said: "There's no need of my talking with him. The girl ran out on us, so it doesn't make much difference why her no-good brother was trailing her. And to make matters worse, she talked the judge and sheriff into turning Chaddiff loose. They've gone somewhere . . . together, I suppose."

"You say Chad's out of jail?" Billy would have jumped up and down with glee if his legs hadn't been roped. "Yip-ee!" he shouted. "Good for Chad."

Goren whirled, his face flashing anger. He strode over and lashed a brutal blow with his gloved hand. It caught Billy across the lips, splitting them and starting a swift flow of blood.

"Keep your mouth shut," Goren hissed.

"You're a mighty brave one," Billy said with mock admiration. "Do you always do your fightin' while you got your man tied down?"

Goren came back with a hard laugh. "I suppose you want me to turn you loose and put a gun in your hand."

"I might want it," Billy agreed imperturbably, "but I ain't expectin' it."

"Then I dare say you won't be surprised when the boys shoot you. Jess, we're on our way to Brent Conners's. We haven't any hold on him now that the girl has skipped. We're going to finish Conners off before he finds out just what's in the wind."

"Shoot him?" asked Jess.

Goren shrugged. "Slick, you come along with us. Maybe I'll have you and Neils ride over to Sixty-Six and get Delling. Jess, you and Hodson stay here and wait for Mapes. He'll be along in a few hours. When he gets here, I want you to head for Conners's. If you should run across Chaddiff or the girl, shoot them."

Long-Haired Jess gulped. "Shoot the gal, too?"

"That's what I said, wasn't it?"

"That's what you said," Jess answered truculently, scratching in his long tangle of hair.

"Any objections?" Goren's voice cut like a whiplash.

Jess hurried to answer: "None at all!"

"Good. I just wanted to make sure that we still understood each other." He pointed at Billy. "And take this fellow out and do away with him. Bury him where nobody will find him. This business has been messed up too much already."

Goren strode away, followed by Slick and the gray-haired man. In another minute the sound of hoofs had faded away outside.

Jess stood in the center of the room, chewing his tobacco and glaring at the door.

"Nice job you have cut out, Jess," Billy remarked. "Do you specialize in shootin' innocent gals? Read about an *hombre* like you one time. Ornery old smoothbore by the handle of Richard the Third. If you've delved into Shakespeare much, you doubtless recollect him. This Richard the Third was sort of hunchbacked and twisted in the belfry. His specialty, as I recollect, was drowning pretty gals in kegs of whiskey."

"Cut the chatter, Buzzard. I ain't shot no gals. . . ."

"You heard your orders, didn't you?"

"I heered 'em," Jess muttered balefully. "I heered an order that had somethin' to do with you, too. How do you hanker to get shot? I'll give you your choice . . . through the forehead or through the heart. I strongly recommend the former as it ain't so messy."

"Wull, that'll take a little cogitatin'."

"Hurry up."

"*Hmm.* What you aim on doin' until Mapes shows up?"

"What difference does that make? Play red dog, I suppose."

"Two men can't play red dog."

"That's true," conceded Jess, scratching his head.

"Sorry you're shootin' me. You see, I was champion red dog player of Yuba City back 'round the year of 'Sixty-One. Thar weren't anybody who could touch me at red dog in them days. I was chucklin' to myself a while back to see how you played the game, Jess. No feel for the more lofty points of the game. But what can you expect from an unlettered buffalo hunter?"

Jess fired up at this and started to argue, then his lips twisted into a wide smile. "Oh, ho! you ain't foolin' me, Buzzard. All that talk . . . you just figure on stallin' the execution.

Hodson spoke up: "Still and all, Jess, he's right about red dog bein' no good for two men. Takes at least three to play it respectable. Fact, I don't know of any good two-handed game, except pinochle, and that takes two decks. You don't reckon we could sort of keep the varmint around for a while if he hankers to play? Goren would never know the difference."

"Don't suppose he would," Jess admitted grudingly, digging at a new spot on his scalp. "I'm willin'. I always was tender-hearted."

"Yip-ee!" applauded Billy. "Been hankerin' all night to teach you boys some rudiments of the game. Cut me loose so I can take a chair."

"Cut you loose? We ain't that crazy. We'll move the table over by the bunk."

"You ought to be safe enough," opined Billy. "Two ag'in' one, and that one without his pistols."

"I aim to be safe. I've heard plenty of stories about you, Buzzard. You're a ring-tailed rangy-tang when you get started, and I ain't aimin' on takin' a chance."

Long-Haired Jess now started scratching his scalp in earnest. Then he made several grabs and came out with a louse that he triumphantly dropped into the candle flame. "My luck must be changin'," he crowed. "I been diggin' around all night for that critter. C'mon, Buzzard. Get your money on the board. We hanker to see what a champeen red dog player acts like."

Billy *clanked* down a handful of gold, silver dollars, and a few crumpled greenbacks. Jess shuffled and dealt. The candle fluttered in the night wind that found its way through the poorly chinked logs. The candle kept getting shorter. Billy raked in the money, turn after turn.

"Ain't they a card you can't top?" wailed Jess. "Do you see through the backs of 'em?"

"Could be." Billy smiled complacently. "You've heard what kind of peepers us buzzards have got."

In another half hour Billy had won all the money. He gave each man $50 for his horse and won that. He won saddles and bridles, and the spurs off their boots, and in the end Jess shoved back his stool and cantankerously rubbed his palm over the butt of a mortgaged six-shooter.

"Reckon the gamblin' men over in Yuba City must have hired you to leave."

"There was an . . . ah . . . committee," Billy admitted. "Leadin' citizens. Sort of an escort of honor, more or less."

"Such luck's an outrage. I ought to shoot you on the spot."

"Hold on now. I treated you boys fair. Where else would you find a man willin' to give fifty dollars for that hoss? He's ring-boned. And them spurs for fifteen dollars! And them ornery old pants of your'n for five!"

"Never mind about my pants. It won't take much procedure to put the ownership of them things right back whar they started. One bullet between the eyes. . . ."

"An Injun trick if I ever heard of one!"

"Hold your temper, Buzzard. We played square with you. You knowed all along we was goin' to shoot you when the game was finished."

Billy sighed. "Reckon that's right. You've been mighty considerate, so I shouldn't complain. But my legs is powerful cramped. Wish I could stretch 'em for a minute. Tell you what. I'll make you one last bet. Win and I get to stretch my legs. Lose and I'll deevulge the secret of how I see right through the backs of the cards."

Jess wavered. Hodson urged him on: "Go ahead, Jess. There's some trick to it. I'd sure like to know how he does it. Just think of what it would mean to us if we won. Look what we could do to that sidewindin' faro dealer in at the Gilded Cage."

Billy wagged his head. "You'd win the gold inlays right out of his southeast bicuspids."

"Sure, Jess, we'd be rich. We'd never have to hire out to var-mints like Goren to do their gunnin' for 'em any more. No more Injun whiskey. Just good old bourbon aged in the wood. There we'd be, layin' around in the shade of some hotel awnin' some place, smokin' two-bit seegars."

"True," conceded Jess. "That is, if we won. But how you goin' to win from a man which sees right through the backs o' the cyards?"

"We'll high card," suggested Billy.

"Sure, let's high card him, Jess."

"Two ag'in' one . . . I call that a fair proposition."

Jess had to admit that it was. He reached across and cut the eight of clubs. Hobson made a couple of nervous starts, then he turned the queen of hearts. Billy stifled a yawn, reached indolently, and turned the ace of diamonds.

"Cut me loose!" he yipped. "Cut me loose, boys, I aim to stretch."

Jess fumed: "You knowed whar it was. Maybe I won't cut you loose after all. No, I ain't goin' to do it. I never could endure a man which would flim-flam his friends at cyards."

"Maybe, if you cut me loose, I'll show you the trick of seein' through the backs of 'em anyhow."

But Jess wasn't listening. He was hauling the double-barreled pistol from its holster. Hodson got hold of his elbow. "Now, Jess, listen to reason. Thar ain't any sense in a man takin' knowledge like that to his grave. It would be low-down criminal, that's what. Let's let him stretch."

"I'd like to stretch his neck." Jess glowered, but he got out his Bowie knife and freed the ropes with a couple of slashes. Billy breathed deeply and stood, slowly, stiffly. He shook one foot, and then the other. Then he settled back on the bunk, picked up the cards, and made several passes with the palms of his hands, stating: "You'll notice I carry nothin' concealed in my hands. Nothin' up my sleeves. Now you spread the cards like this. . . ."

Jess and Hodson held their breaths. Billy rifled the deck and spread it across the table. He settled back a little, and carelessly knocked the candle off the table with his elbow. Its light blinked out. A split second later he slid to the floor.

Jess and Hodson lunged for him, but they found only the empty bunk. He was on the floor between their feet. It took them a second to get their balance, and by that time he had scurried across and grabbed up the Winchester that Hodson had leaned against the wall. It was only another stride outside.

"Thar he is!" bellowed Jess. His double-barreled pistol roared.

A dozen buckshot fanned the air too close to Billy for complacency.

"Don't let him get to the horses!" Jess yelled.

Billy spun and let fly from the hip. The .30-30 slug whipped through the door and plumped into the logs of the far wall. He could hear the two men clawing for cover.

"Dig yore holes, you flea-bit civet cats!" Billy whooped.

His eyes were becoming accustomed to the dark now. There was no moon, but a shaft of starlight revealed a movement near the door. He levered the Winchester and slammed another shot.

He had no more trouble from the house. Jess and Hodson seemed content to remain in its most inaccessible corners. He saddled the best of the three horses, turned the others loose with parting whacks to the rumps, and rode away. The gold pieces in his pockets *jingled* to the rhythm of his horse's hoofs.

VI

I'm another man's wife! These words were the most difficult Mary had ever spoken. She couldn't forget the hurt and the shock in Chad's eyes. The picture of his face stuck in her mind as she headed across the prairie toward a distant notch in the skyline where, Gopher Girl once had told her, Brent Conners's ranch lay. Mary had only a faint recollection of Brent Conners. She remembered him as a tall, smiling man with unruly hair. As a child she had climbed on his knees and pulled that hair—only he wasn't Brent Conners then. He was Harry Raynes. Harry Raynes, her father.

The red faded from the horizon, and dark settled. Even at night there remained a glow that was sufficient to silhouette the notch and keep her on her course. She rode on through the long hours of darkness. At sunup her big bay gelding was picking his way up a barren, rock-strewn hillside with the notch just ahead. It was smaller than it had seemed to be from a distance— just two thirty- or forty-foot cliffs of cracked sand rock encrusted with pink and pearl-gray fungus. In the low divide formed by the notch she sat for a while and looked across the prairie that fell away, infinite miles toward the Big Dry, the Missouri, and the Indian lands beyond. A string of smoke arose in the still air, grayish, almost transparent. She traced it down until she located a cluster of rectangles shining brightly in the morning sun. Ranch buildings. This must be Brent Conners's place.

It seemed quite close in the rare-dry atmosphere, but it took a couple of hours of steady riding to get there. The house was long and rambling, built partly of logs and partly of sawed lumber. Nearby were extensive corrals, some sheds, an old cache house on stilts, and a bunkhouse.

There was no life, no sound, no movement anywhere. She crossed a creek and rode apprehensively across the beaten dirt of the broad ranch yard. She reined in beneath the patchy shade of a box elder and rapped at the door. No answer. She looked inside. What she saw caused her to draw back with an exclamation of horror. A dead man stared at her from the floor.

Her first impulse was to run away—somewhere—anywhere. But a paralysis held her fast. Then, when she did move, it was to go hesitantly on inside the house.

She knew who the dead man was. He was Brent Conners, her father. She remembered him as fair-skinned, young, and with light brown hair, while this man was browned and gray— but still there was something. His gun was still at his hip, so he had not died in a gun battle. He had been shot in the back.

She called for help, well knowing there would be no answer.

Her voice echoed in the empty house. She walked through to the kitchen. A fire had been built in the cook stove, but it was about burned out now. From the rear door she got a view of the corrals, sheds, and bunkhouse.

She called again. It all seemed very quiet—but there was a quiet tenseness in it. A sparrow *chirped* somewhere. A fly droned and beat its head against the windowpane.

She went back to the front room. The feeling came over her that somebody was watching. She tried to dismiss the idea, but it persisted. It grew on her. It became a certainty.

Someone was walking outside in the yard. It was not her imagination. She could hear the steps. And then a broad form shut out the light in the doorway. A man. He leaned casually against the casing and smiled at her. The man was Jud Goren.

"Well, if it isn't little Mary Raynes," he remarked in his oily voice. "You're around early this morning. Sorry I couldn't greet you right when you arrived, but I didn't expect you'd be all alone. I expected Mister Chaddiff would be with you. He must be thoughtless to abandon you after you saved him from the scaffold . . . and in such a self-sacrificing manner. It reminded me of a play I saw one time in Saint Louis."

The fear suddenly left her. It was consumed by her loathing, by her hatred of this smug, overbearing man.

"You . . . murderer."

"Murderer? Why, Mary, isn't that an unpleasant word? I'm sure I don't appreciate being called a murderer." Then the smile dropped from his lips and he strode toward her. "You've forgotten something. You're not necessary to my plans now. Quite the contrary. You're an embarrassment. You're in the way. You know too much. I came here for the purpose of killing that fugitive father of yours and you, too, if I could find you. Well, now I've found you."

"Then why don't you kill me?" she blazed at him.

He considered this for a while, and then the smile returned to his broad, sensual lips. "Why? Because you're too beautiful. I've always had a weakness for beautiful women. Me and Ranquette." He leered. "Remember Ranquette? You should. . . ."

"Keep away from me."

But Goren came closer. Her eyes, darting around the room, came to rest on the revolver at the dead man's hip. She leaped over, dropped to hands and knees, tried to pull it from the holster, but Goren was there with one long stride. He even paused a moment so she could get it free, then he kicked the weapon from her hand. He grasped her wrist and jerked her upright. She struggled, but struggle was futile. She had no idea a person could be so strong. He laughed at her puny efforts.

"Well, you do have fire, don't you? I like my women that way. Women and horses . . . both should have spirit. Did anyone ever tell you that you had spirit? Or how beautiful you are? Ranquette? Did he tell you?"

He twisted her wrist, forcing her close. She could feel his hot breath on her cheek.

"Don't act bashful," he said. "You've been in men's arms before. You were in Ranquette's arms, and he's not as handsome as I. . . ."

Suddenly Goren stopped speaking. He stood erect and listened. A horse's hoofs clip-clopped over stones in the creekbed. He dragged her across the room to where he could look from the door. A rider was just coming into sight over the steep bank leading up from the creek. It was Chad.

She started to scream, but Goren throttled her. She couldn't breathe. Her lungs seemed bursting. Then the blackness spread across her eyeballs and the floor gyrated beneath her feet.

She was unconscious for only a few seconds. When she came to, Chad was only a short distance across the ranch yard. Goren crouched by the window, six-gun in hand, waiting. He cocked the weapon, held it poised for a few seconds, then coolly, deliberately, took a bead. . . .

Mary staggered to her feet, but Goren was so intent that he did not notice. She flung herself toward him. The impact of her body discharged the weapon. Goren cursed and flung her aside, but her hands had closed on the gun barrel. He ripped it away and lashed out with his fist. The blow struck her high on the jaw. She went to the floor and lay still.

Out in the yard, Chad's eyes had caught the first movement in the house. He reined in a trifle. Then a gun *cracked* the clear morning air. A bullet cuffed dirt a few yards in front of him.

Ambush was the first thing that occurred to him, and he was on the point of heading for the protection of the creek. He drove his spurs, and in the same second caught a flash of the struggle that was going on inside. It was now only a short distance to the door.

Goren whirled to face him. Chad saw the six-gun leveled. The roar of it was in his ears as he dived for the floor. The bullet fanned him as it sped by. Goren tried for a second shot, but Chad drove up from the floor, smacking the big man in the middle. They crashed against a long, rough-plank table in the center of the room. The gun flew from Goren's fingers and *clattered* out of sight.

The two men grappled there. Goren was off balance, bent back over the table, so it was a few seconds before his strength could assert itself. Then he set his heels, straightened himself with a *snap* like the spring of a steel trap. Chad was flung back, but he caught himself and whipped a blow to the big man's unguarded jaw. He hesitated, expecting Goren to topple.

Goren smiled. He just stood there and smiled. He didn't flick an eyelash or give a hint that he had felt the blow at all. Then the smile gave way to a sneer, and he asked: "Is that your best punch, cowboy? Did you expect to win with a punch like that?"

Goren came forward, his arms down. He seemed off guard, a set-up for a quick punch, but beneath that seeming carelessness Chad sensed the tenseness of a cat ready to spring.

Then it came. Goren dropped low and charged in. He swept Chad to the wall and pinned him there. He brought up rights and lefts, but they were feeler blows. He was trying for something else. He came close and drove a knee to Chad's groin.

It left Chaw weak and sick. He was dizzy. He dully realized that Goren was setting him up for the kill. He weaved as Goren swung, and took a glancing blow. He clinched and held on. Goren cursed and tried to twist free. As the precious seconds passed, Chad could feel his head clearing and the nausea leaving his abdomen. Goren finally broke away, set himself, and whipped a terrific, smashing left hook. Chad weaved back and the blow missed, carrying Goren off balance. It was a second before he could recover himself, and in that second Chad smashed solid rights and lefts. Goren's head snapped back. He tried to save himself by weaving and throwing another left, but a chair tangled his feet. He hung for a moment helplessly. A savage right connected with his unprotected jaw.

Goren was down over the smashed chair. He kicked himself free and came to hands and knees, shaking his head like a wounded grizzly. He steadied himself, trying to wipe blood from his lips with the back of his hand. He stumbled over Mary's prone form and trod brutally on her. Then he charged, but it was a blind charge. He was no longer the cool, flawless fighting man; he was an enraged gorilla.

Chad shifted to one side, slashing from long range. There was something about the way these blows were landing that sent a thrill of exhilaration through his muscles. He laughed out a challenge. Goren came around and charged once more. But this time Chad did not side-step. He set his heels. His right hand came over with the snap of a bullwhip. Goren went back with doubled knees, his chin pointing to the ceiling. He went down like a beef across the broken chairs.

But by some marvelous resource of energy, Goren pulled to hands and knees. He looked up dully through the tangle of sweaty, dust-mopped hair that strung down over his eyes. He opened his lips, but only a rasping wheeze came out. He crawled out of sight beneath the table.

"Chad!" It was Mary's voice. She had come to and was staring beneath the table. "Chad, he's getting the gun!"

Chad hooked the table with his boot and flung it out of the way. He tried to head Goren off, but the big man pounced on the revolver and came up with it. He backed toward the door. There he steadied himself, holding to the casing, staring at Chad and Mary with bloodshot eyes. He was groggy, but the gun did not tremble. The barrel was trained on Mary's heart. The hammer *clicked* twice as his thumb raked it back.

"Look where you're pointing that!" Chad's voice ripped out.

Goren's lips cracked apart with a snarling, wolfish smile. "What's wrong with how I'm pointing it? Did you think I was going to stop with only killing you, Chaddiff? Do you think I was going to let this girl live? No. She had her chance, and she turned it down. Now she'll find out I'm not the man to sneer at."

As Goren spoke these words, Chad glimpsed a movement down by the creek. A rider came into view. The horse ambled lazily across the soft dirt of the ranch yard. The rider was Billy Buzzard.

"I'll make a bargain with you . . . ," Chad started, angling for time.

"What bargain is there left for you to make?"

"Why do you think I was headed for Starvation City in the first place?" Chad spoke in a loud voice, trying to drown out the sounds of Billy Buzzard's approach. "I have a secret, and there's no use taking it to my grave with me. There's lots of money in it, Goren. If you'll promise to let the girl go, I'll. . . ."

Goren laughed. He started to answer but the sound of the approaching horse made him whirl around. He started the movement that would have brought his gun to play. It was a movement of trained rapidity, but quick as it was, Billy Buzzard was quicker. The .30-30 came to life from the pommel of Billy's saddle; its sharp report cut the air; the bullet *thudded* home.

Goren was knocked off balance. He hung to the door for a second, then his fingers unclasped and the heavy gun *clattered* to the floor. He stared with eyes that no longer hated, with eyes that no longer saw. And he slid forward to the floor.

"Sorry I showed up too late to save your father," Billy said after he had sized things up. "But ridin' the range of the Goren critter was a good morning's work, anyhow."

"How did you know Brent Conners was my father?" Mary asked. "I never told. . . ."

"Shucks, child, a man can put three and three together and get as many shots as there is in a gun, can't he? It's all plain . . . Goren and Mapes was usin' you as a club over Conners so they could hog that Sixty-Six Mile water away from him. Then they figured they could charge fancy prices to north-movin' trail herds. 'Course, I still can't see why you strung along with Goren as long as you did." Mary didn't say anything, so Billy went on: "There's a critter named Ranquette mixed up in this deal somewhere."

"He's my husband!"

Later in the day the Revener rode up with news for Mary.

"I'm sorry to bring bad news, but I have to tell you. Your husband is dead. We found this newspaper in your brother's carpetbag telling about it. He was shot in some kind of a quarrel. Maybe your brother was trailing you so he could give you the news."

Billy chuckled. "By the look on the young lady's face I'd say that widdahood was a mighty welcome condition." He gestured to Chad. "Well, what's holdin' you up? If ever that gal needed a shoulder to lay her head on, it's right now."

Billy went outside and stopped with surprise. Two men had ridden up with the Revener—Sheriff Britt and Old Ben!

"It ain't the resurrection." Ben chuckled. "It's just that us minin' men is tougher than you'd suppose. Takes more'n a Mapes with his Bowie knife to keep me down. I was only wounded that night, and I swam ashore. I'd've been here sooner, only it was a hefty walk in to Starvation City."

The sheriff nudged Goren's body with his toe and looked regretful. "Sort of hoped I'd get a chance to hang that one."

"There's Mapes," Billy reminded him. "You can hang him. Reckon you could go over to Sixty-Six and pick up the whole gang."

Although Billy had led the way outside, he remained near the door, stretching his neck for a view inside.

"What do you see?" demanded the Revener.

"Why, I ain't sure. But from where I stand, it looks like we've gone and lost ourselves a partner . . . to a woman."

ACKNOWLEDGMENTS

"Reckoning at Robber's Roost" first appeared in *Frontier Stories* (Spring, 46). Copyright © 1946 by Fiction House, Inc. Copyright © renewed 1974 by Dan Cushman. Copyright © 2008 by Golden West Literary Agency for restored material.

"The Gambler's Code" under the byline John Starr first appeared in *North-West Romances* (Spring, 49). Copyright © 1949 by Glen-Kel Publishing Company, Inc. Copyright © renewed 1977 by Dan Cushman. Copyright © 2008 by Golden West Literary Agency for restored material.

"The Craft of Ka-yip" first appeared in *North-West Romances* (Fall, 45). Copyright © 1945 by Glen-Kel Publishing Company, Inc. Copyright © renewed 1973 by Dan Cushman. Copyright © 2008 by Golden West Literary Agency for restored material.

"That Buzzard from Brimstone" first appeared in *Six-Gun Western* (6/46). Copyright © 1946 by Trojan Publishing Corporation. Copyright © renewed 1974 by Dan Cushman. Copyright © 2008 by Golden West Literary Agency for restored material.

ABOUT THE AUTHOR

Dan Cushman was born in Osceola, Michigan, and grew up on the Cree Indian Reservation in Montana. He graduated from the University of Montana with a Bachelor of Science degree in 1934 and pursued a career in mining as a prospector, assayer, and geologist before turning to journalism. In the early 1940s his novelette-length stories began appearing regularly in such Fiction House magazines as *North-West Romances* and *Frontier Stories*. Later in the decade his North-Western and Western stories as well as fiction set in the Far East and Africa began appearing in *Action Stories, Adventure,* and *Short Stories*. *Stay Away, Joe,* which first appeared in 1953, is an amusing novel about the mixture, and occasional collision, of Indian culture and Anglo-American culture among the Métis (French Indians) living on a reservation in Montana. The novel became a bestseller and remains a classic to this day, greatly loved especially by Indian peoples for its truthfulness and humor. Yet, while humor became Cushman's hallmark in such later novels as *The Old Copper Collar* (1957) and *Good Bye, Old Dry* (1959), he also produced significant historical fiction in *The Silver Mountain* (1957), concerned with the mining and politics of silver in Montana in the 1890s. This novel won a Spur Award from the Western Writers of America. His fiction remains notable for its breadth, ranging all the way from a story of the cattle frontier in *Tall Wyoming* (1957) to a poignant and memorable portrait of small-town life in Michigan just before

About the Author

the Great War in *The Grand and the Glorious* (1963). *The Rimfire Kid* will be his next Five Star Western.